THE LAS VEGAS LAMBADA

Charlene Torkelson

ISBN:061556450X
ISBN-13:9780615564500

This book is dedicated to all the dancers I have met, all the dancers I have danced with, and all those I have taught. In some form or another you are a part of this book. A piece of you is in each and every character and in each dance performed. You are a special group of people with unique talents. You have and always will be a part of my life. Since the first year I began ballroom dancing, I have worn a small gold band on my little finger signifying my dedication and connection to all the dancers in the world. This book is for all of you who have played such a significant role in my life. Thank you.

THE LAS VEGAS LAMBADA

Tyra Fields settled back into her seat gently pushing the overweight man sleeping next to her back into his space. She tried to look out the tiny window into the darkness of the night hoping to spot any upcoming city lights, but the woman resting in the window seat had partially closed the pull down shade.

She glanced down the aisles spotting Tino Van Arp, another dance teacher traveling to the Dance-o-rama in Las Vegas. He was stretching his long legs out in front of him trying to get into a comfortable position. Several students from the studio were scattered throughout the airplane cabin. This redeye flight had been fully booked, and they were lucky to even get seats aboard. Tyra thought of Edward Garrett, the studio owner seated beyond the curtain in the luxury area. She could only imagine him being waited on hand and foot. Typical! Yes, Edward would be in a cushy comfortable seat with flight attendants bringing him refills of the bubbly. Tyra's thin lips stretched to a straight line hollowing her already sunken cheeks. She was not a beauty, but her classic look was enhanced by pricy outfits, exotic hairstyles, and flawless make-up hiding her freckled face of youth. Tyra expected to be the best and have the best of everything.

This Las Vegas trip was the culmination of hard work.— hard work to improve her dance skills — hard work to claw her way to the top of the profession — hard work to find just the right dance partner. Someone who would look the part. Someone she could mold into the kind of dancer she needed to move her career to the top. She smugly smiled. Little did she know that this trip to Las Vegas would lead to a loss – a loss that could put all of her hard work in jeopardy — a loss that could end her career and her freedom all together.

1

I.

    Tyra Fields sat in her office staring out the door and across the sleek, smooth wooden dance floor. Her claw-like red enamel nails tapped nervously on her desk, her thin lips stretched across her narrow freckled face, and her dark hair fell limply across her forehead brushing the gray wool collar of her perfect suit jacket. Tyra had come a long way since the day she first walked into the dance studio for a job interview. Her intent at the time was to make money – period. To a recent high school graduate schlepping beers at a local bowling alley for the weekly teams in their two toned shoes and colorful buttoned down shirts with names printed on the pockets, anything seemed an improvement. She saw possibilities in the dance business.

    Now she was light years from that skinny kid who wore tight jeans and no make-up. Sophisticated and well dressed, she was still skinny but now she was the manager of the studio. And it was no longer considered "skinny" but rather elegant. She had clawed her way to the top of the chain by some not so nice tactics. Needless to say, Tyra Fields was not a studio favorite. She had made a few enemies along the way. Somehow in all of the intense work to make as much money as she could, she got caught up in the dancing part of the business. She had been bitten by the dance bug and now was beyond the money phase of the studio. She was now intent in becoming the best dancer in the country, and that meant finding the best dance partner.

Her mind debated. What to do? What to do? As she was pondering her problem, she spotted the studio owner, Edward Garrett. Her eyes narrowed. Edward walked in past the front reception desk to his seldom used office. No one was at the desk. Hanging his ankle length camel coat in his office, he returned to the desk. Tapping his finger tips nervously on the top of the desk, he appeared to be annoyed.

"Miss Fields!" he bellowed. "Who is supposed to be at this desk?" His Italian leather slip-ons sounded on the dance floor as he strutted towards Tyra Fields open office door.

Most would be intimidated by Edward Garrett's loudly vocal questions, but Tyra Fields merely leaned back in her chair and smugly stared as he continued to bellow about "service" and "responsibility".

"Sorry, family illness, I believe." Tyra answered with a clipped voice. "I'll take care of any phone calls …when the phone rings, that is. Anyone coming in," she shrugged, "and I'll spot them, run right up, and service, service, service." Her voice dripped with sarcasm. Her smug lips curled.

Edward sputtered, puffing up his chipmunk cheeks making his mustache bristle and his eyes bulge. He clearly was not used to disrespect from his staff. Edward usually had his staff trembling with fear when in one of his moods. This attitude was certainly not something to which he

3

was used to hearing. He huffed loudly, spun around, and returned to his office slamming the door.

Tyra smiled. Edward was a pain to deal with — especially his rule about teacher partnering. He was smart, that was true. He knew when dance teachers began to focus on their own dancing, they changed. They didn't care about teaching more students, more teaching hours, and making more money. They lost interest in making a successful studio, and that was certainly not in Edward's best interest. They began to practice more, find better coaches, and eventually leave the studio to compete and train somewhere else. That was the reason he forbid partnerships among his staff. They could do routines and shows of course, but they had to dance with different people. Tyra was going to change that policy whether Edward Garrett liked it or not! She was going to find a partner right here in this studio – or maybe the studio downtown. It didn't matter. The plan was simple. Tyra was going to find a new teacher – young and green. Then she was going to mold him into the perfect partner. She leaned back again in her chair and smiled. No one stopped Tyra Fields when she had her mind set. No one.

The phone rang. Tyra rolled her eyes. This was an interruption – a bother as she planned her future. It rang again. "Yes?" she answered the phone. She grimaced. She should have answered with the studio name. Next time.

4

It was Mark. Tyra's attention was snapped back to reality. She smiled sweetly and gazed at the framed photo on her polished desktop. It showed a handsome smiling dark haired man holding a young girl. This was Mark and his daughter, a fourth grader from a previous marriage. Tyra winced as Mark asked about her day. "Great," she replied with a cheerful singsong tone to her voice. If only Mark didn't have a daughter. If only her darling Mark liked to dance. She didn't know how much longer she could continue in a relationship with someone who was so removed from her new lifestyle. Mark was a holdback from the bowling alley days. Those days seemed so long ago…so removed.

Tyra crossed her legs dangling her foot up and down. Her soft black leather pump flopped back and forth, the three inch heel clicking lightly on the side of her desk. The roll over line began to ring.

"Sorry, darling, but my other line is ringing." She punched the other line to answer. "Trixie, how are you?" She sounded concerned as she began to page through her date book and responded with a few well placed "uh-huhs". Trixie Appleby was a former student turned receptionist. As she bemoaned her sick condition, Tyra imagined Trixie at the other end of the phone. Trixie was an older woman who tried to look young and fashionable. In spite of a well lined prune-like face, Trixie wore her hair in a straight modern style with a red noticeably dyed color. Her slender body could easily wear the expensive stylish clothing with designer labels she preferred. Today, however, Tyra knew Trixie would

5

be bundled in a puffy soft robe with a box of tissues nearby. She sniffled loudly sounding like a nasal nightmare.

"That's OK, dear. You just stay in bed and get some rest," Tyra rolled her eyes again as if to say, "get on with it." "Don't worry, we'll manage somehow. I'll leave you notes on everything that happens. I promise."

Ashley Arthur sauntered in with his usual flip attitude. Mr. Arthur was not one of Tyra's favorites. In fact, she could barely tolerate the short grinning caramel colored man with his bright shirts, ornate jewelry and crisp fashionable suits. "What's this?" he announced loudly picking through the notes stuck to the sharp tack-like needle with squares of paper perched on top of the reception desk. "They have a new teacher training class starting downtown?" he whined in his nasally toned voice. "Great! Just great! Now I'll have more competition to worry about."

Tyra Fields scurried out from behind her desk and practically sprinted for the front desk. "What was that? What did you say about a training class?" She nudged Ashley out of the way to pick through the notes.

"Right here," he pointed to the note on bright yellow paper. "There was a call from Miss Meeker from the downtown studio asking you to call her about the training class."

Tyra frowned, grabbed the note ripping it from the needle and circled the reception desk. Flopping into the big comfortable desk chair, she peered at the spidery scrawl letting her lips move in silence as she reread the note. She grabbed the phone and dialed. "Miss Meeker, please," she chirped politely.

"Why yes, dear, I notice you have a new training class starting?" She nodded with a slight smile crossing her lips. "How many? Any good prospects?" After a pause and a nod, she continued. "I would love to come down and meet with the class, if I may. Tonight perhaps? Good! Good! I'll see you then, dear." She hung up and smugly grinned as she leaned back in the chair. Ashley Arthur had turned and flounced off toward the teachers' office. His lips pursed tightly and his right eyebrow arched as he flung back the door.

II.

The evening was dark but the streets of the downtown mall were brightly lit as Tyra Fields parked her sports car in the parking ramp and clip-clopped down the street to the new dance studio. Forced to move from the space the studio had occupied for decades at the bottom of the parking ramp elevator, Edward Garrett, the studio owner, had made a quick and possibly ill-advised decision to move the studio to a huge corner space formerly occupied by a large clothing chain that had suddenly and

7

abruptly closed its doors. The space was certainly too large and open for a dance studio. Tyra could only imagine the rent Edward had agreed to pay for a space this size. Entering the front door, she gazed around the spacious area to the dance floor plunked down in the center of the enormous room. "I guess it works," she muttered with a frown. "Certainly not what I would have arranged. But then when have I ever agreed with a decision Edward Garrett has made." She rolled her eyes.

Megan Meeker, the downtown manager, waved from a curiously positioned desk to the side of the dance floor. Miss Meeker had been with the studio for so long, no one on the staff had ever known a studio without her presence. She had a new longer hair-do in a dark purplish hue that matched her eggplant colored dress. Her red lips were so bright they glowed in the dark. Megan eased out from behind the desk and gave Tyra a quick peck on the cheek. They were not friends but tolerated each other.

"So how do you like my new studio?" She waved her hand around the large expanse with pride. "No one can complain they don't have space for a Waltz." She giggled at her own joke. Tyra rolled her eyes but managed a thin lipped smile. "No, they certainly can't." She nodded her agreement.

Turning to gaze at the few people on the floor dancing, Tyra tossed her dark hair away from her eyes and straightened the collar of her gray tweed suit. Her pencil thin matching skirt had a slit up the side revealing her slender legs. Her spiky black heels made her legs appear even longer, and the point on the toes could be considered lethal weapons. She pouted as if sucking on a sour lemon rind and scoured the floor for potential teachers. The whole lot seemed lame – dressed in disheveled worn pants and hand me down ties or dowdy beige skirts. The room certainly was massive. Over in the corner of the room she spotted Karen Danbury. Karen had married into the wealthy socially elite Danbury family. Why she was even teaching dance in this studio was a mystery to everyone. Pushing middle aged status, Karen was no beauty. Her face was pasty and worn with signs of early wrinkles. The hair was atrocious, thought Tyra - ordinary color in a typical mid length cut. But Karen had an eye for fashion. She wore a stunning teal dress that floated as she walked across the floor, and she was standing next to a young blond man dressed in creased black pants and a nicely cut crisp French style white shirt with a sleek black tie.

Tyra pointed to Karen and asked subtly, "A student, I assume?"

"Oh, no," Megan answered back. "That's Cameron Vessi, our newest trainee. Karen is working with him tonight to get him up to speed so he can join the rest of the training class. I interviewed him myself and thought he had great potential." She puffed out her ample chest and smiled.

"Indeed?" Tyra tossed her head again and peered at the couple. He was a might bit short, but cute… no handsome was the correct word. He had a glowing smile that seemed to charm even Karen Danbury. She was blushing a healthy pink color. Most unusual for her, Tyra thought. "I think I'll ask Karen a question or two about my new dance dress. She's so good with fabrics and such." Then she casually walked to the back of the dance floor.

"Miss Danbury, darling," she oozed a greeting as she approached the two.

"Miss Fields," Karen returned flatly. "This is one of our new trainees, Cameron Vessi."

"Charmed, I'm sure," Tyra extended her hand with a flutter of her long lashes. "Karen, I was hoping to speak with you about my new dance dress." She pulled two swatches of fabric out of her small clutch hand bag and displayed them one in each hand.

Karen quickly plucked the two pieces from Tyra's palms and began to study the swatches. "Are you thinking of a smooth dress or a Latin number?" Karen asked feeling the quality of the material.

"I was thinking Latin," Tyra said slowly gazing at Cameron catching his eye and smiling.

"Well, I think I'd go for this one," she said holding up the darker one. "It has more body and would give a sleeker look to a Latin dress. You're thinking of stoning the top?"

"I thought maybe going down into the skirt area and really giving it some sparkle," Tyra turned her attention back to Karen who was now staring at her with a grim face. The glow of a few moments ago was gone. She was aware of the nature of this conversation and began to bristle knowing how this would end. "Thank you for your opinion, Miss Danbury."

Karen didn't reply but quickly excused herself for her hourly five minute break. Tyra reached out for Cameron's arm and asked quickly in a whisper, "Could I have a word with you?"

The two sat at one of the small tables that circled the dance floor. Tyra asked several questions about Cameron's experience here at the studio and waited for him to explain why he had applied for this position. She smiled as if she found it fascinating, but in reality it was the same explanation every new teacher gives. Nothing new or unusual in his words of explanation. Then she started her real reason for the questioning. "I am looking for a male dance partner who really wants to do something spectacular with himself and his career. I want to partner with someone who wants to go all the way to the top in this profession – dance-wise, I mean." She sucked in a deep breath and continued. "I would be willing to pay for all coaching sessions as well as travel to competitions and costuming. You may not know about any or all of what I'm describing at this point in your training, but that is quite a large sum of money. For the success I desire, it is worth every penny. Are you interested in such a lofty goal? Can you imagine yourself as a national champion?" Tyra's eyes glowed as she described the intent of her mission. Cameron gazed at her as she described her dream. She could tell he didn't quite know what she was asking. "This won't be easy, so I don't want you to decide on something this time consuming with too little thought. It will be hard. I can promise you that. It will take effort and sweat and every ounce of determination you have in your body. Do you think you have it in you?"

Cameron smoothed back his thick blond hair with one hand and seemed to ponder her words. His eyes stared into the darkness of the corners of the large space. Certainly, the conversation was a surprise for a new dancer thinking only moments ago of learning a basic Fox Trot step. He was a young man of good manners and tried not to show any emotion at the proposal. He smiled and thanked her for the offer. It was very interesting he said slowly and asked if he could have a few days to think about it. "Certainly," Tyra replied with another flutter of her lashes. "If you have any questions, please call me," she held out a business card with her direct line hand written on the back. "I'm very serious about this offer," she repeated before pulling her hand away from the card as he reached out to accept it. "Very serious," she repeated with breathy emphasis.

Tyra Fields stood and walked across the floor toward Megan Meeker and Karen Danbury huddled near the reception desk. "Thank you, darling, for the advice on the dress fabric. I appreciate your opinion so very much," she gushed waving her fingers at Karen as she exited the studio and pulled her collar up around her neck to protect from the now gusting winds. Clutching her purse to her body, she moved quickly to the parking ramp and her car for the ride back to her studio.

Back inside, Megan turned to watch Tyra Fields glide out the door and then whispered to Karen Danbury. "She's like a lioness ready to pounce on her prey or a Black Widow spider weaving a web for the fly. I don't like it. I don't like it at all."

Karen gritted her teeth. "When I met Cameron Vessi I thought I had been blessed – that I had finally cut a break and had someone who might give my dance career a giant boost. Here is this nice kid with great potential, and I might have the opportunity to finally train a dancer who could dance with me. Me. I would finally be known as a great dancer . A great teacher. And along comes Cruella Deville to snatch him away. It's not fair. It's just not fair at all that she has the power to do this to me. I have never in my life been given credit for anything but what someone else has done. Never me. And I guess now I never will. It's so unfair."

13

Karen's face was stone hard. The anger was struggling to get out, but she would be the ever gracious lady and keep it inside except for this brief confession.

Megan put her arm around Karen's shoulder. "You don't know that just yet. I don't think a decision has been made. It's up to Cameron Vessi."

"Yes, you are right. But how can anyone turn down Tyra Fields. If he does turn her down, she'll make his life hell. Then he'll leave the studio anyway, won't he? Won't he?" Karen turned toward Megan eyebrows raised with a questioning look. "We both know the answer to that one."

Tyra Fields got her call a few days later. Her phone rang around one in the afternoon. Trixie was at the front desk, but the call went directly to Tyra's line. She knew immediately who it was …who it had to be. "Miss Fields here." She answered with a sweetness not normally found in her phone voice. "Why Mr.Vessi, so nice to hear from you!" She listened for a moment and then found her thin lips straighten across her narrow face into a wide smile. "I'm so glad you decided to take me up on my offer. Let's try to get together tomorrow to go over the details. Maybe coffee? Shall we meet at Mario's. It's about half way between the studios – more convenient for both of us. Shall we say ten-ish?"

III.

Edward Garrett was an unusual man. He had incredible charisma, yet few friends and a great many enemies. The reason could be any number of things. It could be his quickly changing moods. Sometimes he was the life of the party and other times he was miserable and depressed. Or it could be his many vices. Yes, Edward Garrett was a womanizer, a drunk, sometimes a druggie, and a spend-aholic. Then of course there was the health food phase when he expected his staff to eat seeds and veggies. That didn't make him a popular companion at parties. Edward could spend more money than anyone. The problem was it was always more than the studios made. To say Edward got himself into some difficult situations was an understatement. He always had problems. And one of his problems at the moment was Tyra Fields.

Sitting at his rarely used desk out in his newer suburban studio, he was seething with rage. He stared at the stark room. Unlike his former lush office in the downtown studio when it was beneath the parking ramp, this small room had a few of his collected primitive masks and paintings from his beloved Jamaica. They gave the room some color, but here the desk was bare – no photos or mementos. It showed nothing of Edward Garrett.

He had put his decorating talents to use in designing this studio. It had originally no character at all – just a large barnlike space. So he had

15

chosen bright showy patterned wallpaper and sleek modern couches –
uncomfortable, but certainly modern – when putting together the reception
area. The small studio beyond the reception desk was floor to ceiling
mirrors with a polished dance floor. Then into the large ballroom - with
not one window to bring in natural lighting - was again floor to ceiling
mirrors. The room was large and the mirrors made it appear even bigger.
The space was not warm and cozy by any means, yet it attracted a crowd
of upper class socialites along with younger corporate singles who wanted
to feel comfortable socially and meet other singles. It was a win-win
situation. But today, Edward was not feeling lucky. He had just learned
Tyra Fields was recruiting a new trainee as a dance partner, and this made
him angry. She knew his rules. She also blatantly knew she was breaking
his rules. There was no misunderstanding on her part. Now he was
preparing for a down and dirty drag out fight with someone who was
making him lots of money. Did he want the money or the power? This
was a sticky situation. His face pinched into a disturbed frown.

He spotted Tyra Fields flutter past his door in a sleek black dress
that clung to her slender body. It was late, and the staff was waiting for
their daily meeting, but he vowed to address the situation immediately.
There would be no meeting.

"Miss Appleby," he bellowed out his door without moving from
his desk.

Trixie Appleby peered over her reading glasses across the top of the reception desk toward the caller and scowled. "Yes, Mr. Garrett?" Her chin dipped, and she stood to lean on the desk so he could see how he had inconvenienced her. But Edward simply closed his eyes and bellowed even louder not noticing her irritation.

"Ask Miss Fields to come into my office at once," he continued. "And tell the staff there will be no meeting today. Tell them to find something constructive to do."

In a few moments with enough time to allow Edward Garrett to heighten his anger, Tyra Fields sauntered into his office with a toss of her sleek hair and regal lift of her head. Her lips curled into an arrogant smile. She nodded a greeting and took a seat, crossing her legs and smoothing her dress as the buttoned front parted to show her muscled thigh. Nothing was said for a few moments. It was as if they both knew what the other was about to say. Finally, Edward Garrett began.

"I heard you recruited a dance partner. A new trainee." He glared across the desk at her. She didn't respond except for a coy smile. "You know my rules about partnering." Normally a reprimand from Edward Garrett would be enough to illicit a bumbling apology from the staff member confronted, but Tyra Fields simply smiled and nodded her head.

Finally, she spoke carefully looking him in the eye with a confident stare. "I have already made an arrangement with the Petersons

17

to train with them in California. That is if you prevent me from partnering with Mr. Vessi right here in this studio. I am more than willing to stay here, and I might add, make you lots of money. Lots of money if you agree to my terms. My ambition is to become a champion dancer. And I can do that here…or there." Her slow and deliberate threat pierced Edward Garrett with a sting.

Edward leaned back in his comfortable chair. He knew the Petersons. They were the reigning smooth and Latin American style champions, but they had recently announced their retirement from competition. They owned several studios in California and would be looking for eager young dancers to train. Tyra Fields and Cameron Vessi would certainly fit into that "eager" category. He had a choice to make. No. He really had no choice, did he? She had him in a predicament. Lose two dancers who could make him money or back off on one principle that he had set years ago before this new competition dance craze would be affecting the rest of his staff eventually anyway. It was something he would be forced to revise in the future – why not now and ensure his moneymaking staff remained intact?

He pursed his lips and leaned forward tapping his nervous fingers on the desk top. "OK. You and your partner have my blessing. No, not my blessing. But you have my reluctant acceptance."

Tyra Fields smiled like a cat who ate the mouse. She always knew she would win. And she had no intention of sitting back meekly when her victory became a reality. She gloated openly. With a gleam in her eye and a haughty leer on her lips, she rose and bid Edward farewell. He slumped back into his chair with a feeling of complete defeat. This was not something Edward had experienced in a long time. Not since his first wife walked out on him when she discovered he was unfaithful. It was the same kick in the gut. And it was not a pleasant feeling. Best to get out of this studio immediately and avoid another conflict. He grabbed his coat to leave.

Trixie Appleby sat across from that closed door with anticipation. She was the heart of the studio – always hearing the latest gossip first. So when Edward Garrett bellowed for Tyra Fields, Trixie knew exactly the reason for the sudden meeting. She patiently waited for the argument – quietly sitting and cocking her head anticipating the loud voices. But there were no voices and no sound of furniture smashing. All was quiet. Suddenly the door swung open, and Tyra swaggered out with a sneer and a look of victory in her eyes. She gave Trixie a wide smile and tapping on the top of the counter informed her she would have dance practices scheduled every morning. "Please note those on the schedule from now on," she stated smugly. "Nine until eleven thirty. Ta-ta." Tyra fluttered her bright red finger tips close to Trixie's face. Trixie once again peered over her reading glasses and frowned. What bothered her most was not knowing – not really knowing what had happened in that closed office. It was a toss-up as to who Trixie wanted to win the battle. Neither deserved it. It was like Godzilla against King Kong. Who to vote for? They were both evil. She shook her head as she penciled through the morning schedules with the new listing. This Cameron Vessi, whoever he was, was certainly in for a shocking experience. He was surely an innocent lamb heading to the slaughter.

Days later when Trixie scurried in a bit early to catch up on some paperwork, her fears became a reality. In the large back ballroom, Tyra Fields was in the height of a screaming fit. She shadowed the doorway with her skinny body dressed in a clinging pair of black dance tights and a baggy sweater widely draping over her shoulders showing pale skin and sharp collar bones. With no make-up and her dark hair pulled up on the top of her head in a pointy shock resembling a fountain, she looked more witchlike than elegant. A poor boy was sweating profusely leaning against a wall. He wore a pair of old sweats and a t-shirt showing his potentially muscular build. He cocked his head and watched the woman in front of him rant. Evidently he had done something wrong. Whatever that err was, he didn't quite seem to understand what it had been. Not surprising with his inexperience. What was she expecting in such a short amount of time? He was still on basics, and she was certainly putting together advanced amalgamations.

Trixie shook her head and slid into her seat. She pulled her multicolored thickly knit sweater around her shoulders. Her ankle length wool army green skirt was expensive and classic. She slid her strappy pewter shoes under the desk and tried to make herself smaller – like a fly on the wall. Tyra paid no attention to the voyeur and ranted all the more. How much more could this boy take before walking out? Trixie simply shook her head again and pulled out the paper she needed to finish but continued to secretly eavesdrop. Maybe I'll have to be a witness to "cruel and unusual punishment" she thought. But Cameron Vessi didn't respond in a negative way. He listened and listened some more.

"That's it for the day!" Tyra screeched in an earsplitting voice. Mr. Vessi shrugged and walked off the floor. "Don't you dare walk away from me," she screamed at his back.

"The honeymoon is over I see," Trixie commented softly as he walked past the desk. Surprised at first by her presence, he stopped and turned peering at her eyes behind the sliding reading glasses.

"There never was a honeymoon, believe me," he said, then he grinned, and Trixie chuckled back with a knowing nod.

Trixie made a point to get to the studio just a bit earlier than usual each of the next few days. The soap opera conversations she heard were delightful, and she found herself enjoying herself way too much. But that didn't stop her from pulling into that parking lot just a little before the end

21

of their practice. Today, Edward Garrett also arrived at the studio earlier than usual. Edward was not one to ever arrive early for anything, so his presence surprised Trixie.

"So our golden boy should be about ready to quit, I would guess," he commented as he leaned against the front desk. "He probably realizes by now that he's out of his league." He chuckled wickedly.

"Actually, I think Cameron Vessi is a saint – and he has no intention of letting that witch get the better of him. He will never quit is my prediction." Trixie Appleby let her glasses slide down her nose. "And I think he has every intention of becoming a better dancer than she is. I think she's met her match."

Edward Garrett frowned at this assessment just as Ashley Arthur skipped in. "Oh, Mr. Garrett, I think I have a wonderful idea for our Las Vegas staff routine."

Las Vegas was the venue each year for the annual Dance-O-Rama that drew dancers from all over the United States for a week of dancing and partying. The Minneapolis studios always performed a staff routine – another of Edward Garrett's rules. He seemed intent on showcasing his studio and making life beforehand miserable for his dancers with daily practices. His routines were always unique.

Edward growled. "What is this 'wonderful idea' of yours?" Edward prided himself in choreographing something so new and unusual that other studios really took notice.

"A Lambada," Ashley pronounced crisply. "I saw a Lambada last night in a local Latin club that was wild. It's a little known dance from South America that is so hot and sexy it would be hard to teach, but wonderful to perform." Then he began to demonstrate a little of the basic step with a grind of the hips and a dreamy closed eye expression.

Edward grimaced, but watched intently. After a moment or two, his expression softened. He twisted his lips and leaned back for a better look. "You know, you might have a good idea there. Any suggestions for music?"

"I might have a few ideas," Ashley said slowly almost in disbelief that Edward Garrett was actually interested in this crazy idea of his. That was the key, he decided. It was crazy.

Cameron Vessi walked briskly toward the front desk with Tyra Fields scurrying along behind him. She would have been screaming in his ear, but she spotted the group chatting at the front desk and instead pasted a plastic smile across her face.

"So how is everything going?" Edward asked politely.

"Wonderfully. Just wonderfully," Tyra returned with chipper tone to her voice and a pasty curl of her lips. Cameron simply nodded. His face showed no hint of emotion – neither painful nor delighted. He certainly was a master of his emotions noted Trixie as she gazed into his face.

"That's just great!" Edward said slapping Cameron on the back and grinning at Tyra. She spotted the sarcasm immediately and glared for a brief second before catching herself and turning it into a triumphant smile.

"We'll be ready to compete at the Las Vegas Dance-O-Rama," she announced in a chatty manner.

"Really? That soon. Marvelous." Edward's words were dripping with honey. He could hardly wait to see their routine. It would be a pleasure to see them fall flat on their faces in front of the world.

Tyra's face hardened as she flounced off to change her clothes and prepare for the daily meeting. Cameron watched her walk away with a blank stare. It was evident he was trying to formulate an opinion of the woman, and it wasn't quite coming together. He was the kind of person who genuinely liked everyone, but what about Tyra Fields? She was a hard person to like. He seemed to be trying hard to find the good in her. Was there good in Tyra? Trixie thought quickly and then tried to put that negative catty thought from her mind.

24

Ashley and Edward were in a corner further discussing the Lambada. Edward was listening intently to Ashley's explanation, and Ashley loved to talk so he was enjoying himself immensely. Ashley Arthur's short body seemed pudgy compared to Edward's lean slender form. Arthur had on a pair of pleated pants in a charcoal gray with a silky shirt in a textured fabric and brightly patterned thin tie. His round glasses made his face seem wider. Edward was patting his curly toupee and gazing at himself in the mirror. His elegant silk blue suit was perfect. His patterned pink, blue and gray tie was expensive. His flat soft leather Italian pumps looked both comfortable and fashionable.

Trixie rolled her eyes at the whole scene. It was days like today that made her wonder why she was here in this studio with these strange but interesting characters. The Lambada? Las Vegas?

IV.

Megan Meeker sat behind the reception desk tapping her toe. The studio was empty for the moment, and she gazed around at the enormous space. This building had been a large department store before Edward Garrett took over the location. The outside was lined with large plate glass windows allowing the business crowd to stare in as they passed each day to and from their job to their car or bus. It was wonderful advertising but a little intimidating for beginning dancers not wanting to be the

25

entertainment for the passers-by. The dance floor looked like a postage stamp on an envelope – it looked tiny compared to the surrounding empty space. Edward's idea to use such a large space for a dance studio was interesting but not practical in the least.

Megan stared at the schedule for the day. It was relatively full, but she needed to block out some time to work with the new trainees. They could be trusted to work on their own for a few hours if they had something tangible to work on. She had given them assignments geared to their own dance abilities, and they knew they would have to take their series of tests before they could even think about teaching and making money. That was the stumbling block for most perspective teachers. They had to train and work hard to get to the level of beginning teacher. It was not easy. Some of the new trainees would be included in the staff routine Edward would be starting today. He actually thought it would be ready for Las Vegas in five weeks. That might be a practical timeline for a seasoned dancer, but these newbees were going to have a few weeks of hell to keep up. Maybe they would be consumed during their studio time with the Lambada. That was what she was going to have to do. Keep them practicing this ridiculous routine over and over until they looked like they were actually professionals like the rest of them.

Teachers began to arrive, drop their gear back along the wall - their new designated staff office. Staff from both studios would be meeting each morning for rehearsal. Cameron Vessi was changing into dance shoes. He was one of the few new trainees who even had dance shoes. Then again he had to in his new partnership with Tyra Fields. When would those two practice now that Edward had called these special staff sessions? She began to feel sorry for the poor boy. And he never, never complained. Megan shook her head. She was lucky to have him. Would she be able to keep him for her staff or would Tyra snap him up claiming partner rights? Again she shook her head and found her teeth grinding angrily.

Tyra fluttered in like a winged bird in a wind storm. Her hair flowed back and her silky skirt swirled around her legs. She greeted Megan with a wave and a kiss on the cheek then began to throw her bag next to the reception desk as she grabbed for a pair of strappy Latin dance shoes. "So how is everything going?" She took a quick look around the room and spotted Cameron talking with a slender new dark haired trainee.

"So who's that?" she asked crisply tossing her head toward the pair in the back corner of the dance floor.

"Well, you know Cameron of course, and the young lady is one of our trainees, Jordan Jensen." Megan glanced toward the pair at the end of Tyra's stare.

"I don't recall seeing her when I was here previously," Tyra looked the woman up and down. She had a dancer's body with a slight turn out of her feet, narrow hips and lean arms. Her dark hair was long and slightly curled framing a classic face. "Is she any good?"

"Not bad for a beginner. She has potential," Megan nodded.

Tyra smiled faintly. "Good. Good." Then she turned and paused with no expression for a long moment.

"People, people!" Edward clapped his hands and drew the staff around him into the middle of the dance floor. He explained the idea of the Lambada routine and motioned for Ashley to turn on the music. The music was a rhythmic instrumental with a sensual feel. Edward's hips began to gyrate automatically to the beat of the music as his body naturally moved in place. His mind seemed totally absorbed in the music.

Placing the staff around the floor, he paired people by height. Tyra was partnered with Tino Van Arp, a tall slim Latin-looking dancer. Karen Danbury was dancing with Carl Young. And Cameron was partnered with new trainee Jordan Jensen. Tyra glared at the two as they chit chatted in the corner. Tino grabbed Tyra's hand, and she grimaced pulling away then rolling her eyes when he snarled back. They ignored each other for a few moments as Edward demonstrated the first few movements of the routine. Ashley smiled with delight as he put his arm over his partner's shoulder.

Edward watched the rehearsal with a huff and then with a wave of the hand split up Cameron and Jordan. "You two are too new to dance together," he explained and put Karen with Cameron. He pushed Jordan into the eager waiting arms of Carl Young. Carl was always ready to work with a new trainee. And that was the problem. As much as Edward hated to send the lamb into the arms of the wolf, he had no choice. It was a matter of putting the experienced dancer with someone inexperienced. That's the way it had to be done.

"Miss Meeker, we need costumes. What can you come up with for all of these people?" He swept his arm toward the dancing group. "It has to be Latin style and something that says 'Lambada'."

"And what does 'Lambada' say to you?" Megan leaned over the desk top with a smirk and gazed at the choreography the group was demonstrating.

"It is very sensual. Hot. You know. Not high and crisp like a Cha Cha, but down and grinding." He began to sway his hips and move up and down.

"I see," Megan answered pressing her lips tightly together. "Is this the dance I should have my new trainees learning first thing? Is this a good idea? I mean isn't a simple Waltz or Rumba a better idea?"

"Believe me. This routine will be the talk of Las Vegas. So what can you find for us?" Edward waved his hand through the air with a flamboyant gesture.

"Let me look around. Maybe a colorful short ruffled skirt with a short blousy top in another bright fabric. Some large flowers for the ladies hair perhaps? And the men with black Latin pants and matching ruffled shirts? How does that sound?" Megan surveyed the dance again and began to write down a few notes on a pad.

"Good. That sounds good. How long for you to find something?" Edward liked the ideas she had.

"I'll start working on it right away. Can I get some measurements today?" She pulled out a measuring tape from her desk draw – a well used piece of dance equipment for Megan.

He nodded. "Tyra! That part has to roll, baby. Show her again Mr. Arthur. Yes, yes. That's more like it!" Edward turned to Megan with a gleam in his eye. "I am so excited by this routine. People are going to be blown away. There has never been anything like this before. I am going to be known as the magic man of dance." A huge grin spread across his face. He was like a kid at Christmas. His shoulders shook, and he danced around in a tight circle. "The magic man of dance! I like it." He licked his lips.

Two and a half hours was just about enough time for a first rehearsal. The group was tired. Some grabbed bags and sauntered off to change. Others grabbed water bottles and leaned against the back walls. Tyra Fields sank into a chair behind the reception desk. Even daily rehearsals with Cameron hadn't prepared her physically for today, and she felt worn out. A different dance took its toll on her body. Her hips and legs ached from the down and up movements of the Lambada.

"So Tyra, when are you and Cameron rehearsing with this Lambada routine taking up your mornings?" Megan looked up from her schedule to glance in Tyra's direction.

"I guess after evening lessons. Around eleven or so. Cameron will have to drive out to my studio after hours, and it's going to be late nights from now on." She sighed at the thought.

"I could let him leave early," Megan offered quietly. "Time spent rehearsing will be almost more worthwhile than practice here with novice trainees."

Tyra's eyes lit up. Her head snapped toward Megan. "You would do that?" Then her face shifted from skeptical to grateful. "Thank you. Thank you," she repeated.

Hum, thought Megan. I've never seen Tyra Fields show a soft side. I guess I just did. She watched Tyra leave the studio with a smile on her face. Then Megan walked across the floor to Jordan and Cameron who had once again joined in conversation. "Hey, Mr. Vessi," she called out. "I am going to let you leave the studio early each evening so you can get to your rehearsals with Tyra."

"You dance with Miss Fields?" Jordan fluttered her long lashes as she tilted her chin down and gazed up at Cameron. Cameron was not a tall man, but he seemed like a giant in comparison to the tiny Jordan Jensen.

He didn't know if Jordan was impressed with his dance partner or jealous. Cameron hadn't known either one of them for very long, but he was beginning to feel caught in the middle of two women he didn't really understand. He had suspected that Tyra was only interested in him as a dance partner – he was her ticket to reaching a goal as a dance champion. And Jordan... he didn't know what she wanted. She was just a nice person, or was she? How should he answer her question? Plowing right in, he looked down at Jordan and answered, "Yes, Miss Fields and I are dance partners. We are getting ready to compete for the first time in Las Vegas."

"Wow, that's impressive. I'm so glad I'll be there to see you perform," she smiled up at him and tilted her head again to the side letting her hair fall across her forehead.

"Right now it's pretty time consuming..."

Megan Meeker left the two of them discussing rehearsal times and Las Vegas. She shook her head. Typical new trainees she thought. The dance business sucks you in – it drags you down and can drown you if you let it. She knew from personal experience that sometimes a dancer had to separate from other dancers before the studio becomes suffocating. They would learn soon enough.

Tyra Fields stomped into the studio with a huff. Trixie Appleby lifted the phone to signal Tyra she had a call. "It's Mark," she called out as Tyra walked past with not so much as a nod.

"What!" Tyra screamed into the phone as Trixie gasped. "Second line!" Trixie called out loudly waving frantically. Tyra had just screamed at a potential new student trying to schedule a first appointment.

Tyra glared across the dance floor and punched in the second line. "I told you, I don't have time right now. In fact, I think we should take a breather. Yes, that's exactly what I mean. Not see each other for a while. Las Vegas is too important for me to worry about you and your problems. Yes, I see everything about you as a problem." Then she slammed the phone down and picked up the photo on her desk and hurled it across the room shattering the glass into shards on the floor. She stomped out of the office to find a broom.

"Must have been some rehearsal…" Trixie sighed raising her sharply plucked eyebrows and letting the reading glasses slide down her

33

nose. Then after calming down the woman on the other end of the phone and actually scheduling an appointment for a lesson, she patted herself on the back for dealing with an impossible situation. She slowly walked around the desk and headed to Tyra's office. Standing in the doorway, she folded her arms and demanded, "OK, what's going on here?"

Tyra looked up from kneeling in the corner with a dust pan full of glass. "What are you babbling about?" Tyra's voice was harsh.

"Don't take that tone with me, young lady." Trixie's voice became sharp as she suddenly became a mother. "You just screamed at Mark. And you've been about as kind as a rattlesnake lately – not to say that you are normally sweet. But it's a little uglier than usual. So tell me what's going on and tell me the truth." Her body blocked the doorway, and she glared down her nose with an air of authority.

Tyra sucked in a breath of air and smugly crossed her arms across her chest. "I think I'm falling for that snot nosed partner of mine." She rolled her eyes and exhaled noisily in frustration.

"Cameron?" Trixie looked puzzled. "So what's the problem other than he's young?"

"We just came from rehearsal – Edward's Lambada routine, and I think Cameron is interested in someone. And that someone is not me." Tyra shivered. "I don't know why that bothers me exactly. But it makes me crazy. How can I practice with him, care about him, and know that he doesn't care about me? That's the question."

"Well, I wouldn't be so sure he doesn't have feelings for you. But the way you treat him would make me believe you must be right. Who in his right mind would see you as anything but a complete bitch?" Trixie didn't mince words. She told her exactly what was on her mind.

"Whoa. That was brutal." Tyra's shoulders slumped forward. She paused to consider those words. "True, but brutal." She nodded her head slowly.

"I know it will be hard for you if not impossible, but you need to change your ways if you want anything but animosity. That means actually being nice to him and no screeching. Smile. Be sweet. Oh, no. He'll suspect something is wrong…" Trixie let a sly smile cross her face. Let it sink in, let it sink in she told herself as she continued to smile waiting for a reaction from her boss.

"Humph." Tyra pouted. "I guess you're right of course. I'll have to wear a rubber band on my wrist for this one."

"Rubber band?" Trixie questioned.

"Yes. If you need to break a habit or remind yourself of something, wear a snappy rubber band on your wrist and every time that bad habit comes up, snap your wrist. The sting will remind you what you set as your goal. It works. Really!" Tyra nodded convincingly.

"Well we'll have to see how sore your wrist is after a day or two, won't we?" Trixie suggested with a point of her finger. "And remember, it takes sugar not vinegar to attract the bee."

Tyra Fields growled then dumped the dustpan of glass shards into her wastebasket. Dropping into her chair, she whipped open her top drawer and snagged a thick rubber band. Staring at Trixie still covering her doorway, she slipped it on her wrist and gave it a good hard snap. "Ouch!" But her look of pain and anger quickly changed to a slow devious grin. Then she gave it another snap. "Thanks!"

The next few weeks at rehearsals both for the Lambada and the professional championship proved to be startlingly different. Tyra Fields was so upbeat and delightful that even Edward Garrett noticed.

"What's with Susie Sunshine?" he asked Trixie one day as Tyra pranced by the desk with a smile plastered to her face. "She's been unusually accommodating, surprisingly cheerful, and extremely helpful during rehearsals. It's absolutely shocking, and I might add quite sickening." He peered over the reception desk at Trixie as she recorded lessons taken the previous day. She looked up over her glasses and pursed her lips.

"I guess she's in love." Trixie whispered with a raise of her eyebrow.

"I didn't think that was possible for Miss Fields. Are you sure? Who is it? Not that young kid she's dancing with? He's practically in a different generation than she is." He huffed.

"Hasn't stopped you." Trixie glared into his eyes as he tried to release himself from that gaze but couldn't seem to avoid it. She continued to glare as his cheeks puffed up and reddened to an angry blush.

"Touché`, my dear," he grimaced.

"I must say you deserved that one." Trixie wasn't afraid to tell Edward just what she thought. "And Cameron Vessi seems like someone any woman could fall for. He's handsome and sweet. There aren't many who fit both profiles."

Edward Garrett turned abruptly and walked back to his office. "Certainly not you," Trixie muttered to herself when she saw him sharply shut his door.

Tyra Fields strutted across the dance floor to the reception desk to check her schedule. Her thin smile spread like a tight ribbon across her face. The rubber band on her wrist hung loosely.

"I see your wrist is nice and white – no red marks!" Trixie remarked as Tyra placed her hands on the desk top and leaned over to stare at the booking sheet.

"It was easier than I thought it would be," she said cheerfully.

"Must be working," Trixie prompted waiting for a return comment.

"It is…it is," Tyra smiled back with a twinkle in her eye. "Make sure you mark me out for the Las Vegas trip. Cameron and I will be heading out earlier than the rest of the staff so we can do our preliminary competition. We'll compete in the Rising Star categories in both smooth and rhythm. I'm hoping for maybe a top ten finish if we're lucky." She smiled again. "You have to start somewhere."

"You seem to have a good attitude about this whole competition thing," Trixie was surprised to hear the sparkle in her voice.

"It's all coming together much better than I expected. Cameron is a quick learner even though he is inexperienced and really a beginner. He is so determined and very talented."

Trixie nodded with surprise. This coming from Tyra Fields! She was actually complimenting someone else. Maybe this rubber band thing had actually made a change in her whole persona. "I might have to try this rubber band thing myself," she commented as Tyra headed back to her office with a light bounce to her step.

Tyra piled her bags in the reception area. Four matching leather bags in a bright but soothing red tone stacked neatly with a garment bag that looked like a stuffed mushroom hanging on the coat rack next to the pile. Cameron stood in the doorway nervously checking his watch. He knew better than to rush Tyra. She hugged her staff as they wished her good luck and seemed to be trying her best to stay on time. "We'll see you in a few days," she waved as she hoisted two bags and handed the rest to Cameron. He looked more and more like a pack horse as she swung another bag across his back.

"Break a leg," called out one teacher with a pump of his fist.

Trixie knew this was a first. Tyra and Cameron were the first to compete in a professional competition. Edward Garrett was strict with his rule and now it was broken forever. They would be the test case. They would be the ones to demonstrate what could happen when two paired up as partners. Would they stay with the studio or was Edward right in his fears? The next few weeks would be the test – the go ahead for future couplings or the return of a tried and true rule. Trixie shook her head and wondered. Her questions would soon be answered in a very different way than she could ever imagine.

V.

True to her word, Tyra called the studio each day to report their hits and misses – and there were many of each. Tyra and Cameron had made some mistakes in the rhythm competition not even making it through the preliminary cuts. Tyra's voice showed her disappointment when she replayed that first time out on the floor. Both had showed their nervousness she reported. That was kind thought Trixie. She hadn't blamed Cameron's newness. She had shared the responsibility for the failure. That was big of her thought Trixie.

But the second day had gone much better. Their first preliminaries for the smooth division had gone very well. They had made it to the second level. Tyra was very pleased. Her voice was enthusiastic and looking forward to the following day and a second time to shine. And shine they did. They actually won their heat and were going on to the final round. Ten couples were chosen for this round. Just to make it that far was amazing. Tyra's call was guarded but excited.

The rest of the staff would be in Las Vegas for the finals. Trixie of course would stay back in the studio and keep the business running smoothly. Edward was gathering together his dancers at the studio and getting ready for the taxi ride to the airport. They each grabbed their bag and carry-on holding their costume as Trixie called out after them, "Call me as soon as they dance!"

"What about after we dance?" called back Ashley. "What about our Lambada?"

"Call me after that as well," Trixie waved them off. "Hot, hot, hot!" She smiled at her own fashionable rhetoric.

The studio was quiet. Trixie stood up from her comfortable desk chair and sauntered over to the stereo system. Music would help. She put on some music that wasn't really dance music but more of an easy listening jazz. It broke the silence. She got her work done quickly and looked around for something to do. This was an unusual moment. She couldn't remember a time over the past year when she hadn't been extremely busy. It was rather pleasant.

The music was so soothing, she leaned back in her chair and closed her eyes. The phone broke the silence. "They took third!" the excited voice of Ashley screeched through the phone.

"What?" Trixie knew third was unthinkable. Ashley repeated himself.

"It was amazing. They didn't look the least bit nervous. Cameron was strong and virile in his tuxedo. Superb! Tyra looked darling in that floating caramel colored dress that Karen designed for her. It looked elegant yet dynamic – really eye catching out on the floor with all that stone work. It simply glistened as the lights caught the facets. Tyra's hair was tre-chic! She had it up in a twist…" Ashley went on and on.

"OK. Enough of what they were wearing. Get to the dancing," Trixie finally demanded.

"Oh, my. The dancing! They were perfection. I was surprised they didn't take second actually. The top couple... well, no one could have touched them. They were absolutely amazing. But Cameron and Tyra simply floated across that floor. You would not have believed their Waltz. Divine. Absolutely divine." Ashley gushed. "When they called out the tenth placed couple, Cameron and Tyra were ready to head on up to the podium, but it was someone else's name called. And so forth. Then, when they announced them as the third place couple, the room positively exploded. The screams were earsplitting. I could hardly even hear anything over my own shrieking voice." Here Ashley took a breath and sighed loudly. "Tyra was almost on the floor. Cameron had to hold her up as they presented them with their trophy. I think she was in shock! Absolute shock! Oh, and the Lambada went well, too."

"You already danced the Lambada?" Trixie checked her watch. It was still early in Las Vegas.

"It was hot. We smoked. All those hips grinding and shaking. The crowd went wild. Of course, in a matter of seconds it was over. Gone. All that work," Ashley's whinny voice complained.

"You'll perform it over and over again if Edward has anything to say about it," Trixie promised.

42

"I'm sure we will," Ashley laughed. "We'll see you sometime tomorrow. Chao!"

Trixie expected Tyra would call shortly. So she waited patiently but no more calls came in. She sighed. "Thank goodness for Ashley," Trixie thought as she locked the front door and scurried out to the parking lot. She thought about the staff in warm sunny Las Vegas as she felt the sting of sleet whip her face. Minnesota winters were hard to deal with sometimes... no, not sometimes. Always.

The next morning, Trixie was in early. She could hardly wait for the teachers to return so she could get more of the story. But the story she heard was not the one she expected.

Trixie gazed at herself in the mirror. She was slender for a woman of sixty and well dressed. Her black dress was expensive and chic. It was a clingy knit with lacy loops at the wrists and hem. She wore a chunky piece of colorful purple glass around her stringy thin neck. Her face was lined and gaunt with colorful cheeks from the pink blush she stroked below her puffy bagged eyes. She smiled and tossed her sleek bangs and stick straight hair. The quiet of the studio was deafening. Trixie tingled with anticipation for the return of her noisy cohorts.

The first one in was Tyra Fields. She practically walked on air with a smile across her face that was neither plastic nor fake. Rushing to

43

meet her, Trixie gave her a big hug and congratulations. Tyra glowed with excitement.

"Now, honey, tell me all about it," Trixie pleaded. She wasn't wearing her glasses but gazed down her nose as if the frames would fall off any minute.

"Well," Tyra began breathlessly. "It was all so surreal. We didn't do well in the Latin dance preliminary. I got my foot caught in my dress during the Rumba, and I practically fell on my face right away. We stumbled through each of our routines. So when it came to the smooth dances, we knew it was time to step it up. We went out and killed! I think Cameron has found his forte with the smooth dances. He floats across the floor with ease. What footwork he has! Then the award. That was really something in a dream. I can hardly remember the Lambada with all the excitement over the professional competition. People simply mobbed us. It was delightful. So delightful in fact that we got married."

"You what?" Trixie stammered falling back away from Tyra clutching her heart with her hands. "Repeat that please."

"We got married," Tyra said simply. "It was Las Vegas after all. There were all kinds of wedding chapels so we picked one and did it." It was all so matter of fact.

Trixie staggered backwards and sat right down into one of the reception room chairs. It felt hard to breathe all of a sudden.

"Oh it was a marvelous few days. Such a competition and then the wedding. And Karen..." Tyra continued.

"Karen?" Trixie looked confused. "Karen Danbury?"

"Yes, Karen. She had so many requests for costumes and dresses after everyone saw the one she designed for me, that she quit."

"Quit? What do you mean she quit?" Trixie was breathing even harder than before.

"She decided to stay in Las Vegas and design dresses. It was her calling, I guess. The one she designed for our smooth dances was amazing out on that floor. I had no idea it could twirl so beautifully," at that Tyra spun around as if she were still in that dress. Her hair floated out behind her, and Trixie felt as if she were watching a movie in slow motion.

"What will her husband say to all of this?" Trixie asked in a squeaky voice.

"Oh, I hadn't thought about him. Hummm. Well, I'm sure they will deal with that. He's quite wealthy you know. Maybe they've even discussed the possibility before this trip. Who knows? Anyway. Miss

45

Meaker and I need to get together sometime today to discuss staff. We're going to divide up the training class. The downtown studio will need a replacement for Karen ASAP. She really taught a huge bulk of their advanced students, and Megan will have to find someone who is ready to take her place." By this time Tyra was simply rambling. She was moving from one situation to the next. "I don't know who we'll get out here. I'm hoping for Cameron of course, but Edward might nix that idea. You know how much he was against dance partnerships? Well, I'm sure he's just as adamant about married couples teaching together. What do you think?"

Trixie grabbed her heart again and stared blankly into space. This was not the story she was expecting to hear. The world was tumbling, and she began to feel like she was Alice falling down the rabbit hole. Trophies? Weddings? People quitting? Wow! This was too much to take. She could hardly wait for Edward Garrett to come in – oh, maybe he wouldn't even show up. The downtown studio most certainly needed him more today than they did. Her eyes blinked wildly.

"Well, ta-ta. I'm off to meet with Megan. I'll have more news for you when I return." Quickly, Tyra turned and flounced out the door with a flutter of her fingers. Trixie stayed in the comfy chair for a few more minutes letting the words sink in. The world was turning upside down.

Tyra and Megan sat across from each other in Megan's small but cozy office. The space had been partitioned off from the main spacious

46

dance area for conferences and meetings with students. Tyra crossed her long lanky legs and leaned back with a pasted on smile that infuriated Megan to no end. Smug. That's what it was – smug.

"I'm certainly not going to let you have Cameron. Edward would never allow that," Megan stated with a flat matter-of-fact tone.

"Agreed. I know he won't allow that. Now that I've bridged that gap for the rest of you…" Tyra didn't look Megan in the eye but focused on her newly polished nails.

"What do you mean by that exactly?" Megan's voice was haughty and tinged of anger.

"I mean our wedding. Now that we've bridged that issue having one staff member marry another staff member."

"I see. You don't mean making my most productive teacher quit abruptly with no warning. I think that is an issue we should 'bridge', don't you?" Megan's face was beginning to turn colors. Her voice was becoming labored.

"You blame me for that?" Tyra leaned forward with wide eyed innocence.

"I certainly do. You took Karen's dance partner from her. Then you took that partner to Las Vegas, happened through some lucky draw to win third place and to top it off, you married him!" Megan's face was livid.

"Karen is an old hag who is already married. What does she want with a young dancer like Cameron Vessi?" Tyra huffed.

"This is not about romance. This is about career. You stripped her of her chance for a promising dance career. And not only that, you took away our most financially successful teacher. Now what will this studio do?" Megan Meeker let her words split the air in daggered sharpness.

"You mean, what will you do? What will Miss Megan Meeker do?" Tyra's voice dripped with sarcasm. She taunted again, "What will Miss Meeker do?" Her face contorted like a young bully stalking his weakling victim.

"Miss Meeker will turn this studio into a huge money-maker with the best staff ever seen. Miss Meeker will take Cameron Vessi and Jordan Jensen and Carl Young and turn this studio into the top studio in the country, that's what Miss Meeker will do." She stood and leaned over the seated Tyra with venom in her voice. "You…you can take that clodhopper over there for your studio." She pointed out to a gangly male dancer who was struggling with the basic tango step. He picked up his large feet giving his movement across the floor a bouncing effect. Tyra sighed and rolled her eyes. Of course, this is just what she had expected.

Megan Meeker moved back away from Tyra. She stood still and gazed across the room for a long time. Megan's new short hairdo was cut in a sleek contemporary style with a tinge of purple. She wore a vivid blue dress with a tightly belted waistline. Megan always looked perfect. Her burrowing stare was uncomfortable.

"You, know for a while I thought you had changed. You began to treat people with more dignity and respect. But I now know a leopard doesn't change its spots. And you haven't changed yours either. You'll always be a slithering snake waiting to strike at some innocent prey. I hope to God Cameron knows what he's getting into. Or maybe he's the prey. I certainly hope not." Then Megan turned and walked out of her own office. She needed a cup of coffee – and quickly.

Tyra slunk out of the studio peering over her shoulder at her new husband staring from the corner of the dance floor. Cameron was practicing dance moves with Jordan Jensen, the new teacher Megan planned to make her new star money maker. Jordan was slim and tiny with a mass of curly dark hair. Today she had the right side pulled up. Jordan could be a beautiful young woman but still had a college girl look to her wearing well worn dresses and skirts that were slightly out of date. She had a softness around the edges appearance that drew people to her look and personality. Cameron looked up from dancing the Mambo to see his new wife saunter out the door. He frowned and stood silently for a moment. Then he was drawn back into the dance by Jordan who tugged at his elbow regaining his attention.

VI.

Edward Garrett was livid as expected with the changes Las Vegas had produced. He had a long dragged out discussion with Tyra Fields that ended with the usual walk out. Nothing was resolved, and nothing changed. Edward was a hot air balloon who bellowed but seldom took action. Trixie Appleby watched it all from her fortress front desk. What had she done? Her intention to suggest Tyra use honey in her tactics had worked too well she was afraid. Deep inside she felt guilt. It was as if she had created a monster. But the extent of that destruction was just beginning to surface.

Cameron came out every morning for rehearsals in the suburban studio. They were able to return to their usual schedule now that the Lambada was finished. But the rehearsals were very different than they had been. They had quickly turned into shouting matches between the two newlyweds. Tyra, the experienced dancer wanted to control the flow of the practices while Cameron was beginning to feel more self confident with his dance abilities and wanted a say in the choreography. Tyra found this infuriating. Trixie was afraid there might be a physical altercation.

Not that she blamed Cameron. Who wouldn't be driven to insanity by Tyra Fields?

This particular morning, the two were bantering back and forth as usual when Trixie arrived. She slung her coat across her chair and tried not to listen but the voices became louder wafting from the back ballroom. "I don't understand why you need to stay so late rehearsing?" Tyra's voice sounded crisp.

Cameron shot back with a softer response. "I'm doing some routines for the dance parties. You know that's part of the system. You and I rehearse each morning. The only time I have is after work. You understand that. I know you do."

Then there was a crash, and Trixie realized Tyra had thrown something across the room. Obviously Tyra didn't understand. Cameron walked out of the ballroom shaking his head and dragging his workout bag. Trixie saw sadness in his eyes. He didn't even look up as he passed her.

A week later everything blew up. Cameron and Jordan were practicing late. The studio was very public with windows along the main street. As they danced, late night patrons from the downtown bars and dance clubs would stare through the window. The outside darkness hid the streets from the lit dance floor. So although it seemed to the dancers that they were alone, they never were. Someone had evidently called Tyra

51

about these "dance rehearsals". She stood watching outside as they swirled around the floor clinging to each other, lingering in certain positions, and eventually nuzzling each other. Standing back so her image wasn't visible to those inside, Tyra waited for almost an hour until the two wandered to a shadow along the back wall. She felt so hot the cold air couldn't penetrate as her breath steamed into the darkness of the night. She waited another half an hour waiting for them to return to the floor. When they didn't she began to bang on the door.

Cameron looked out spotting Tyra's dark silhouette at the door. She began to make more and more noise until he finally let her in. She stalked back to the shadow and dragged a half clothed Jordan out onto the floor. "What is the meaning of this?" Tyra demanded with an angry curl of her thin lip. Jordan shrunk lower in fear. She had never directly come in contact with Tyra Fields. Tyra had been her hero when she started training at the studio. It never quite connected that Tyra was also Cameron's wife. Well, tonight that thought suddenly occurred to her.

"I'm sorry. I'm sorry," Jordan whimpered keeping her eyes to the floor. Tyra turned and pointed at Cameron. "What have you done?"

Cameron buried his head in his hands. He wanted to protect Jordan, but the guilt was overwhelming. This wasn't about his relationship with Tyra, it was about throwing Jordan into hell. It was what he was doing to Jordan that made him feel guilt — not what his adulterous affair meant to Tyra.

"Tyra, please. Let's go home. You and I need to talk this over. Just the two of us," he said with calmness in his voice. Tyra exploded. She sputtered and screamed with clenched fists. "Please, calm down Tyra. This is between you and me." He tried to grab her hands — hold her fists but she swung and clipped him in the jaw. She swung again and hit his shoulder.

Suddenly Cameron found his voice. He stood to his full height and said, "Stop!" He grabbed both her hands and said in a steady voice, "We are going home. Now."

The two of them left, Cameron trailing behind Tyra leaving Jordan Jensen cowering on the floor. Tyra moved crisply and sharply but let Cameron open the door for her and follow her down the street to her car. "How much do you want this partnership?" he was asking her. "How much do you want me to stay with you?" The words seemed to snap her back to reality. What did she want? Was she willing to let this dance partnership end?

The next afternoon Tyra Fields stalked into the downtown studio. Megan Meeker was at the front desk, and she rolled her eyes when she saw her at the door anticipating the worst. Megan gripped the edge of the desk. Cameron had filled her in on the evening's events. He confessed to

Megan he and Jordan had been having an affair but it was over now. He and Tyra had smoothed out their relationship. That was that. Those were Cameron's words. Now here was Tyra Fields walking into her studio and no good could come from this visit. Megan shook her head and waited for the explosion. And it certainly came as expected.

Tyra walked stiffly onto the dance floor and pointed at Jordan Jensen who was teaching an older gentleman. Pointing her finger she demanded, "I want this home wrecker fired this minute!" Her voice flooded the open aired space like an echo bouncing off the walls.

Jordan Jensen's face went pale and suddenly she fell to the floor in a crumpled heap. She had fainted. The elderly balding student immediately bent down to feel for her pulse. His face turned toward Tyra Fields with shock and horror. Suddenly, Tyra realized what she had done and backed up. She looked over her shoulder towards Megan and with a hiss repeated, "I want her fired. Now!" Then she turned and left.

The ambulance siren sounded in the distance. Jordan Jensen was put on a stretcher and carried out to the waiting vehicle. Cameron Vessi had been in the back area set aside for the staff. He rushed out to see Tyra walking out and Jordan rolled onto the stretcher. His face searched for Megan Meeker. "What should I do?" was the question his face asked. Megan quickly moved to Cameron's side. "Go in the ambulance," she nodded. "You know you want to go. So go. I won't breathe a word to

Tyra. I promise." Cameron didn't go in the ambulance. He followed the ambulance in his car. That was the end of Jordan Jensen — a promising dancer who got in the middle of a stormy relationship. She was a dancer who had possibly found her Prince Charming but would lose him forever. It was a simple case of wrong time, wrong place. Would they ever meet again when the time was right? Would this Juliet ever see her Romeo again?

Megan Meeker would have to search for another advanced teacher to train. She found that person in Annalea Montgomery, a sweet young tap dancer who happened to wander into the studio the following week asking about employment opportunities. In spite of finding a new talent, Megan Meeker would never forgive Tyra Fields for destroying two promising careers.

VII.

Tyra Fields seemed determined to return to her sickening sweet ways. Maybe the affair had given her a change of heart. Trixie found it hard to believe such a cold heart could warm that much. It was possible, but highly unlikely. She came in early to see the two of them — Tyra and Cameron — actually smiling and joking after their rehearsal.

"Oh my, that was a strenuous rehearsal!" Tyra was commenting with a laugh. "We'll have to have more of those." She smiled with a playful gleam in her eye. "I'm even feeling sore. Wow, I could certainly use a massage."

"That sounds good, doesn't it?" Cameron replied smiling.

"Well, you two are in luck," Trixie stood up waving a coupon. "We have a new masseuse in the mall who dropped off discount coupons the other day. You'll have to take advantage of this opportunity."

"Discount coupons?" Tyra ran up and snatched the paper from Trixie's fingers. Her eyes scanned the print. "Wow that is a great deal. Why don't you call and make an appointment for me sometime around my lunch hour? I guess you'll have to wait for your massage, my dear." Tyra looked teasingly at Cameron.

He sighed. "You'll have to tell me how it feels. Maybe I can schedule for next week when my days are not quite so busy. With fewer teachers I have to teach most of the couples. I'm booked up."

"Great! You're making money. You might soon be my bread winner…" Tyra spouted and then saw the look of shock on his face. "Oh, I'm sorry. I didn't mean you don't support us. You do, you do. How inconsiderate of me to make that suggestion!" Her voice trailed off. She was trying, Trixie thought. It was just hard for her to be a normal caring person. Her tongue got the best of her. It frequently fluttered without much thought. Trixie shook her head.

Tyra came back from her massage with raving reviews and a new glow.

"Did you get your lunch?" Trixie asked.

"I'm not really hungry," Tyra admitted. "I haven't been feeling that well lately. I don't know … a bug or something."

A few moments later Tyra stormed out of her office like a fleeing mouse scurrying along the wall to the rest room. She came out a few moments later with a pasty white look on her face.

"What's wrong? You looked so good just a few minutes ago after your massage?" Trixie peered over the desktop with concern on her lined face. She swept a wisp of hair away from her glass frames and let them slide down her nose so she could get a better look.

"I threw up – and I had nothing in my stomach to come up. Sorry, that was gross. I don't know what is wrong with me. I have no appetite and seem to want to head to the bathroom all the time." She huffed out a breath trying to pat her cheeks back to a healthy color.

"Might I suggest you take a test?" Trixie rolled her eyes.

"What kind of test?"

"A pregnancy test." Trixie frowned back at the glazed over look on Tyra's face.

"Oh no. It couldn't be…" Tyra opened and shut her mouth then grabbed her coat to head down to the pharmacy at the end of the street. "Let's get this over with right now." She stomped out with an air of disgust and tightly pressed lips.

An hour later, Tyra was sitting behind the desk with Trixie. Tyra was resting her head on Trixie's shoulder and curling up in her arms.

"Now, now. It's not that bad," Trixie was cooing. "Let an experienced mother give you a bit of advice …"

"What's this? I'm hoping it's not a new romance sprouting." Edward Garrett growled as he unbuttoned his long ankle length camel coat and checked the messages on the spindle.

"Mr. Garrett," Tyra rose. "I need to speak to you for a few minutes."

"I'm hoping this isn't bad news," he snarled.

"Well, I hope it's good news. I mean. It may seem to be bad news at the moment to me, but I'm thinking it might be …well, good. At least Trixie tells me it's good. I'll reserve my judgment on it for say maybe a year or so." Tyra rambled on as Edward stared at her with a curious glare.

Trixie sat at the front desk trying to appear busy, smiling at the teachers as they entered, and twisting her thin mouth into an awkward worried purse. Her reading glasses were put on, then off, then on again as the minutes ticked by. "Just work on your schedules for the day," she suggested when one of the teachers asked about the daily meeting. The group meandered back and forth between the teachers' office and the back ballroom. Tino Van Arp put on some music and began to choreograph a few patterns for his evening group class.

After an hour Trixie watched the office door fly open, and Edward Garrett strut out to the front desk. He had a plastic smile on his face that made his cheeks round and his right eyebrow raise slightly.

Trixie nodded and whispered, "How are things going?"

Edward smiled a more natural smile and pondered before answering. "They are fine." He nodded and added, "Just fine." Then he let go of a chuckle letting Trixie know that he was accepting of the news – probably much more so than the uptight Tyra Fields. Even with the door almost closed, Trixie could hear a muffled sob from within. The music engulfed any sounds and allowed Edward to gather the teachers for a brief meeting. He led them to the back ballroom and closed the double doors. Trixie watched the procession and quickly scurried around the desk as soon as the doors shut to rap lightly on the door. Without waiting for a reply Trixie entered and knelt in front of Tyra.

"He was fine. Actually, it was surprising," Tyra's voice was a scratchy breathy whisper.

"He usually understands crisis quite well. It's the easy daily things that throw him for a loop," Trixie commented with a nod of her head. "My knees are killing me. I'm an old lady. Mind if I take this seat?" She motioned to the chair next to Tyra.

"You are going to be OK. I know it doesn't seem that way right now, but it is a truth. In another year or two, you won't even remember you had this kind of anxiety. You'll have a whole new set of feelings, believe me." Trixie laughed and moved her face closer to Tyra's. She couldn't help but notice the swollen eyes and gray color of her cheeks. "Perk up. You still have to tell Cameron. What do you think he will say?"

Tyra let out a puff of air. "Whoa, I haven't even thought of Cameron." She rolled her eyes and began to grimace.

"So… you haven't even thought about Cameron?" My, my thought Trixie. What does this say about their relationship? She is worried about Edward Garrett, her own competition schedule and her career but doesn't remember Cameron? Hmmm. A leopard doesn't change her spots, and Tyra Fields doesn't change hers either. The spots were still all there. Tyra was and would always be herself. Just for a moment, Trixie felt sad — sad for Cameron and sad for this new baby.

60

Edward Garrett didn't reveal anything to the staff. Life went on as usual. Cameron seemed to take the news with his usual ease and cheeriness. Tyra and Cameron continued to rehearse as usual but the intensity seemed to unconsciously lower to a less complicated level. Trixie found the whole atmosphere to be surprisingly calmer and less tense. Even with the concern for the pregnancy, Trixie found herself smiling more and laughing more frequently. She began to enjoy her job and looked forward to coming to work.

"Hey, Cameron." Trixie called the handsome man in his comfortable black athletic pants and clingy t-shirt to the desk after a morning rehearsal. "I still have this coupon for a massage. Want me to schedule an appointment?" She held up the colorful square and let the corners flutter as she waved it close to his sweaty face. His smile was brilliant and so genuine. She could see he appreciated her effort to make life better. He nodded. She picked up the phone and checked the number on the coupon. "Next Wednesday. Great! He'll be there at eleven sharp. Thanks."

Cameron's face showed his appreciation as he snagged his workout bag and waved on his way out the door. "Thanks. I love you." He pointed a finger and winked over his shoulder.

Tyra continued to look pale. Morning sickness was becoming a common daily occurrence. Right before rehearsal was spent in the

61

bathroom and again right after. She would come out with a soulful roll of her eyes and a new appreciation for saltine crackers. Trixie would put a few on her desk whenever she spotted the quick trip to the back of the ballroom.

"How do you know about these things?" Tyra sighed as she nibbled on a corner leaning back in her comfy chair with her shoes kicked to the corner of the office.

"Just wait until you're a mom. You'll know about a whole lot more than you ever expected possible than when it's just you." Trixie scooped up the shoes and moved them over to an out of the way spot behind the desk. "Moms know a lot about life. I scheduled Cameron for a massage tomorrow after rehearsal by the way. So keep tomorrow shorter if possible. I know he can really use that luxury. It's been a long few weeks for him."

Tyra twisted her mouth for a moment but stopped short of making a smart remark. She wanted to make a comment about how much more she had taken than Cameron, but she held her tongue and internalized her discontent at Trixie's sympathy for Cameron. Trixie could see Tyra's thoughts. It was evident in her eyes. The narrowing slant of the eyes for just that short flash of time and the dark shadow of discontent was not missed by Trixie's quick eye. Tyra smiled a sly slow grin and nodded her approval. "Of course, Cameron really needs a relaxing massage." She popped the last of the cracker into her mouth and let loose a little shiver. "I'd better get changed quickly. Shoo, shoo!" She fluttered her fingers and turned her face away with a barely noticeable scowl. But Trixie didn't miss the gesture and made a mental note.

The next morning after rehearsal, Cameron's face was glowing with anticipation of a relaxing massage. He grinned at Trixie and gushed his thanks. Tyra followed him to the front desk and waved her good-by as he bounced out the door. "Well, how was I?" she said with a sarcastic tone pressing her lower lip out into a angry pout and a quick about face on her heel retreating to her office. The door slammed sharply, and Trixie was left sitting with an empty hollow feeling in the pit of her stomach.

"Try to do something nice for someone..." she shook her head and began to record the lessons taken the previous evening. The task was tedious and time consuming. When she finished she always rewarded herself with a chocolate from her drawer. It was a daily treat she looked forward to and marked the start of the new day. Trixie leaned back and closed her eyes enjoying the flavor of the chocolate in her mouth and the completion of a dubious task.

The phone rang. She let it ring once and a second time before answering in her most professional voice. "Dance studio, may I help you?" Pause. "Yes, this is Miss Appleby... Oh, my. Could you repeat that, please? Yes, I understand. I'll take care of this right away."

Trixie put down the phone and immediately called Megan Meeker. "We have a problem…"

VIII.

While Cameron Vessi enjoyed his massage, there was an earth shattering consequence of this relaxing endeavor. The masseuse had found a disturbing lump. He had suggested Cameron see a doctor to determine the extent of this growth. But after this quick and calm consultation with Cameron, he had made a call to Miss Appleby to give a more detailed warning. He told her it was imperative to get Mr. Vessi to a doctor immediately. He suspected the diagnosis to be more shocking than he had imparted to the young Cameron Vessi. Trixie had quickly told Megan Meeker about the concerns and the two scheduled an emergency doctor's appointment. Despite Cameron's protests, Megan took him right away to the doctor and then to the hospital. It was a rare but deadly cancer that needed treatment immediately. Now it was Trixie Appleby's task to tell Tyra Fields and Edward Garrett the shocking news.

The days passed. Tyra Fields' belly began to grow round like a bump on a thin twig. Worse than the added protrusion were the daily visits to the hospital. Now instead of a morning rehearsal, Tyra spent the hours visiting Cameron. Around noon each day Tyra would slowly and sluggishly drag herself through the reception area of the studio to her office. Trixie would watch her slow procession with heartfelt sadness.

"How is he?" Trixie would ask every day in a polite tone.

"He's fine," Tyra would answer in a sad somber tone. Then she would quietly shut the door coming out only to give the meeting at one o'clock.

Each day during the meeting, Trixie would make a call to Cameron. "Hi handsome," she would begin, and he would laugh.

"So how is the meeting going? I told Tyra to focus on goal setting today. How does that sound to you?" he would respond. Cameron's voice was always cheerful and hopeful.

"Sounds good to me," Trixie would reply in return. "So how are you feeling today?"

Some days she could hear a catch in his voice as he would respond with a positive comment. Some days he sounded tired. Other days he just changed the subject, talking instead about how beautiful Tyra looked with her little belly sticking out a bit more. Today he sighed and said, "How do you think I feel? I have tubes coming out of my stomach and doctors poking and prodding me with confused looks on their faces. What should I think about it all? I don't know. I just don't know."

Trixie put the phone down and slumped back into her chair. Then she lifted the phone and called the hospital again – this time a call to the doctor. She needed a few answers.

"Well, I don't mean to be the bearer of bad news, but this type of cancer is usually quite simple to detect and treat. Cameron Vessi is a young healthy man who should be the perfect patient — a quick cure. But for some reason, he is not responding to the usual treatments. We are at a loss as to what to try next. And Mrs. Vessi seems to be in no condition to be a support to her husband. She seems to be dealing with her pregnancy without much excitement." His bedside manner was not sympathetic.

"And how would you deal with an unplanned pregnancy and a husband who is possibly deathly ill? Maybe you deal with sickness and death every day, but we don't. This is rather a new concept for us." Trixie's voice was crisp and rather angry.

"I'm sorry. I guess I sound heartless. I'm really not. But it would certainly help Cameron if he had someone who was encouraging rather than so…so self centered. I doubt if it helps him to have someone always complaining. That isn't a medical opinion. It's personal," he was blunt and to the point.

"I see. I think we can try to give him a little more support and positive feedback if that would help," Trixie's voice softened.

"I think that would be very helpful. Now I must go. I have a busy day." And he hung up abruptly.

Trixie stared at the large daily schedule spread out on the desktop and pondered the next move. "Hello Megan? We need to talk." The two of them arranged a visitation schedule with each staff member taking a turn at visiting the hospital. Cameron seemed to perk up with all of the new attention he was receiving. Soon he was able to leave the hospital for home.

Megan called Trixie with the news. Cameron would be teaching a few hours each day. He looked like "death warmed over" she reported, but his gaunt appearance and thinning hair didn't seem to bother his ever faithful students who clambered to make sure they were somewhere on the short schedule he currently had. "It's a joy to have him back," Megan reported. "He is constantly smiling and joking. It's a pleasure to be around him."

Trixie smiled as she listened gazing across the dance floor at a brooding Tyra seated at her desk with feet propped up on a stool, a puffy pillow cushioning her swelling ankles. Tyra Field's down turned lips and darkening circles under her eyes worried Trixie.

Placing the phone back in the cradle, Trixie sauntered across the dance floor to Tyra's office door. She stood in the archway for a few seconds and then cleared her throat. "You know when I was pregnant with both of my children, I simply stopped doing everything about the eighth month. It was just too difficult. All that extra weight and feeling so tired. You need more rest — especially with all the other things you have been dealing with. Don't be a martyr. Go home and take it easy!" She stared at Tyra who looked down at the floor for a minute then lifted her eyes in a sorrowful puppy dog expression. "Go home!" Trixie ordered.

Tyra slowly rose, sighed deeply, and grabbing her purse waddled toward the door. "I'll check in with you daily," Trixie waved in a sing-songy voice. "Finally…" she muttered under her breath as she continued to wave.

Cameron Vessi always seemed upbeat and cheerful, reporting on Tyra's growing belly each day with a glint in his eye. But he gradually grew weaker and more tired. He had to sit down occasionally during a lesson, but his students just smiled patiently and enjoyed his presence. It was as if they appreciated each and every moment he had for them, and he certainly enjoyed them.

Mrs. Crawford brought a huge plate of homemade cookies for Cameron saying, "You need to fatten up a bit!" And others brought him fruit or other assorted treats. He graciously accepted the gifts and tactfully placed them out on the front desk for the staff to sample. Cameron didn't seem to add any weight, but the rest of the teachers began to notice a few extra pounds around their middles. "Dance it off," he would say when they complained about their fatter bellies. Then he would add, "You have no idea what a fat belly really looks like." He laughed heartily and tried to imitate Tyra walking.

Trixie called Tyra every day and reported on the pertinent stats such as the number of new students, teaching hours and money taken in. Tyra seemed pleased with the calls but only answered with a few "hums" and "yeahs" in a quiet disinterested voice when the numbers were given. She was clearly away from the studio both mentally and physically in her own little world. So when Trixie called with her report and Tyra had seemed winded when she answered the phone, Trixie knew it was only a matter of a few days before the baby's arrival. "I was just cleaning out the bathroom and vacuuming the living room," she reported when asked about her breathless voice. "Better get ready," Trixie thought with a smile. "This is it."

Indeed, a few short days later, Megan called with news that Cameron had been called off a lesson to get over to the hospital immediately. Tyra was having her baby. All who were free, quickly hurried to the hospital to await the arrival of little Macy Jasmine Vessi. At seven pounds, she had a tuft of dark hair like Tyra and a sparkle in her blue eyes like Cameron. She was beautiful.

Cameron smiled proudly and gave Tyra a peck on the cheek which she quickly brushed away with a tired wave of her hand. Then after cradling Macy in his arms, he handed the bundle to the nurse and lowered himself to a chair next to the bed. He leaned back and let his eyelids slowly close. The excitement in the air was electric with Megan shooing the staff out into the waiting room so Tyra could get some much needed rest.

Some of the teachers moved through the hallway to the nursery to ooh and aah over the new baby. Others sat in the hallway chatting eagerly and sipping cups of coffee. The next moment was horrific. There was a scream from behind the door. A group of nurses pushed past the group and into Tyra's room. The door remained ajar as Megan and Trixie peaked in pushing back the curious teachers crowding toward the door. A gurney was pushed quickly down the hall and into the room. A moment later, Cameron Vessi was wheeled out. The nurses' faces said it all. There was no hope. He had died. Cameron Vessi was dead.

After consoling Tyra, Trixie managed to grab Cameron's doctor for a short conversation. He ushered her into an empty room and sighed deeply. "Cameron knew he had very little time, left, but he desperately wanted to see his new baby. We could have kept him in the hospital until the end, but he chose to live rather than vegetate. He loved his dancing, his students, his staff, and his family. So we let him leave for his final days. I promised him I wouldn't tell anyone. That was his wish." The doctor was direct, and Trixie knew truthful. That would have been Cameron's wish. It would have been too stressful for Tyra to have the burden of knowing Cameron only had a short time left to live. Trixie nodded and let the doctor leave the room.

Edward Garrett hadn't been at the hospital during this time, but in this moment of great tragedy, he stepped up to make a few crucial decisions. He met with the mortuary and Cameron's mother to plan the funeral. Surprisingly, he made the choice to wait until Tyra was home and feeling stronger to schedule the date. His heart was showing — what little heart he normally seemed to have was here and now evident.

The service was held in the mortuary a week later. The parking lot was filled to overflowing almost an hour before the service was to begin. Students and teachers from the cities as well as other studios across the Midwest came to pay tribute to a young and well liked dancer. It was somber. He had died too young, and they all felt the loss to the dancing community. Instead of the usual dancing and merriment these people experienced daily, this moment was dark and morose. That is until Edward Garrett stood up before the crowd. With people standing in the back and spilling out into the hall, Edward began to smile. "Cameron Vessi would not want anyone to be sorrowful during this day when we celebrate his life. So let's get out of this sad mood and show Mr. Vessi how much we loved and appreciated his talents and his amazing personality." With that, a photo of Cameron dancing with Tyra flashed on the wall and a lively Samba began to surround the silence in the room. The crowd looked up at a smiling young man with a full head of blond hair gazing at the woman he loved. He was alive and vibrant, gifted and charming, and bright with personality – not a body in a wooden box anymore.

The crowd began to move their hips and shimmy their shoulders to the beat of the music. Suddenly the mood had shifted from depressing to upbeat. Trixie began to smile. Who would have thought Edward Garrett was capable of such a sensible speech. And then she remembered this was definitely part of Mr. Garrett's charisma and charm that peeked through the cracks when needed on those rare occasions when no one else could verbalize what was deep in the heart. Yes, he was an amazing person sometimes. But those times were too infrequent. Anyway, today he came through in a big way, and Cameron Vessi's funeral was a happy and fitting tribute to the life of a great dancer and even more dynamic human being. "Thank you, Mr. Garrett," Trixie whispered under her breath as she joined the festive event.

IX.

It took a while before things got back to a normal semblance of order. Tyra stayed home for a few weeks, but was itching to get back to the studio and her dancing. Sitting home alone with a newborn and the memories of a newly departed husband certainly was not easy. Luckily, her own parents and Cameron's mother were always around to help care for Macy and give Tyra time to grieve. But Trixie's daily calls soon became a more lively discussion about Tyra's future and her need to get back in shape. They discussed the usual losing weight subject and of course, the exercise.

"Will I ever get back to my old dancing shape?" Tyra now confided in another mom – and there were so few on the dance studio staff. Her voice almost whined in desperation.

"Of course, dear," Trixie replied. "I remember…" and she took a few moments to replay her own weight loss concerns after the birth of her own children. Then she added, "We're missing you here in the studio. We really are. The one o'clock meetings are really rather blah with Edward. Not that he isn't interesting, but most of his subjects are just not as applicable to every day lessons as your topics always are. We sort of leave with a sense of confusion asking ourselves just what he said for that hour."

Tyra laughed. "I'll admit, caring for a baby can be rather boring. And I really can't wait sometimes to have an adult conversation."

My, my thought Trixie. She's actually sounding normal. "Just wait!" she responded back. "When they begin their walking and talking and toddler antics, you'll really need a few adult hours for relief. Not to say it's not fun to see their new stages… It's just different. You'll see."

"I'll try to get myself acclimated to getting back to studio life. Although it will seem strange to be there without Cameron," Tyra's voice began to trail. "I guess I haven't let myself think about that. It will be hard." Suddenly she just stopped talking and the silence was deadening.

A moment later, Trixie signed off and sat back to rethink the whole conversation. How could they make this transition easy? Oh, that wasn't going to happen. It wouldn't be easy by any means. And it wasn't.

Tyra breezed into the studio in a slim body and new hairdo. Her dark hair was now dyed a bright platinum blond. It floated behind her just like the skirt of her brightly flowered dress. She had a new set of shiny red nails and vivacious color to her make-up. Her gold strappy shoes accented her red toenails. This certainly wasn't a grieving widow. Trixie sat back with a start before moving out from behind the desk to give her a welcome back hug.

The other teachers spilled out from the office to greet their manager. Tino Van Arp stood back and whistled. "Wow, lady, you look terrific!" he complimented as Ashley Arthur elbowed him in the ribs. "What?" Tino turned to glare at Ashley. Ashley simply rolled his eyes in disgust.

"Lady?" Ashley whispered then repeated "Lady?" He turned and stalked away with a shake of his head.

Tino Van Arp was a tall slender man of Latin ancestry. His dark complexion and glistening black hair was considered extremely handsome. Most women turned to watch him when he passed. He was definitely a standout in a crowd, but his demeanor could be crude and offensive. He stared again at Tyra Fields with a twist of his mouth that turned up into a sly grin.

Tyra opened her office door and looked quickly around the space with a cheerful appreciation. "Ah, it's good to be home again," she said in a quiet tone. She slid behind her desk and touched each pen and piece of paper on her desk with a light tap and a nod. Then she carefully slid a framed photo out of her purse and set it gently on her desktop. It was a picture of little Macy in a lacy pink dress with a baby headband of pink flowers haloing her dark shock of hair.

There was a gentle rap on her door, and she looked up to see Tino Van Arp peering through the glass siding of the door. She frowned briefly and then called out, "Come in."

He sauntered in and stood by the chair placed in front of the desk. "I suppose you are wondering what I'm doing here," he began with a smirk. After a silent nod from Tyra, he continued. "I know you are going to try to find a partner soon. I want to apply for that position."

"And how do you know I am going to want a new partner?" Tyra asked with a tilt of her head. Her new blond tresses hung down across her cheek, and she brushed it back with a flick of her freshly manicured hand.

"Because winning dance competitions is addictive for you, and you need a win to feel complete. I'm the man to get you to that goal. I want the same thing you do." He leaned down resting his hands firmly on her desk so he could better stare into her face.

"I see." She turned her head and began to finger a pen with one hand as the other began to tap lightly on the top of the glistening wood surface. "Maybe you are right. Maybe I am looking for *another* win." She emphasized the word "another". "Why are you the one I should partner with? I'm sure there will be many offers coming in for that position very soon. After all, my name is well known in the dance competition world."

"I work hard. I'm here and available. And I know the kind of person you are."

"What exactly do you mean by that?" Tyra eyes narrowed and stared directly into Tino's smiling face.

"You are a complete bitch." Tino's smile didn't move a muscle.

Tyra reeled back in surprise. "What? What are you talking about you sli…."

He cut her off before she could spew a series of names in his directions. "You are a difficult person to deal with. You yell, you throw things, you complain about everything…need I go on. Everyone at Cameron's funeral was thinking the same thing. They were wondering what a saint like Vessi was doing with a bitch like you. But I knew. He knew you were a hard working dancer who didn't stop at anything to reach the top. Isn't that what you told him right from the start? That's what I heard. The rumors were true, weren't they? You got to the top with him, and now you can get to the top with me." He grinned and cocked his head to the right side. "I'm good. I truly am."

Tyra frowned. It was blunt but struck a nerve. Truth. That's what struck the nerve. "So you think you're good, do you? Well, let's see what you got, boy." She dragged out a southern drawl and leaned forward with a glint in her eye. "Let's see what you got. Show me."

Now Tino frowned and leaned back putting his hands on his narrow hips. He turned, opened the door, and held it open with a slight bow waiting for Tyra Fields to follow him out to the dance floor.

"Oh, not with me, my dear. Choose your partner. I'll watch…" She smiled wickedly and passing through the door, grabbed a chair, and slid it into the corner. Taking her seat, Tyra crossed her legs and let her gold sandal bob up and down. She crossed her arms and leaned back with her own smirk. Now it was her turn to gloat.

Tino looked around quickly pursing his lips. Who would be the right partner? Jordan Jensen walked through the ballroom heading toward the front desk. She was not an experienced competition dancer, but he had danced frequently with her lately as she tried to move from the beginning dance department – working with new students – into the back department and the advanced students. He knew she would look good. "Jordan," he called out and motioned for her to come toward him.

Jordan looked around curiously. The last time she had come in contact directly with Tyra Fields had not been pleasant. Shortly after Tyra left on her maternity leave, Jordan had come back to the studio and was now teaching here in the suburban location. Edward Garrett had listened sympathetically to her story and hired her back on the spot. Now she was doing quite well for herself. She hoped her new shorter haircut and more businesslike attire would not trigger recognition of who she was in Tyra's mind. Jordan had hoped to fly beneath the radar for at least a little while before Tyra remembered the incident with Cameron. Turning her head away from Tyra and focusing on Tino, she listened carefully to Tino's request. His eyes pleaded. Dance with him? Now? Sure, why not?

The music began. Tino and Jordan started out with a fast, crisp Cha Cha. Then they moved skillfully into a bouncy Samba. Tino led Jordan into a series of Compasos before going into a quick Mambo. The Latin dances were definitely Tino's forte.

78

Tyra tried to show a bored reaction. Then she motioned for them to move on. "I want to see some smooth dances, please." She waved her hand toward the person standing by the music equipment. Instantly a slow Waltz swirled through the ballroom. Tino took Jordan into his arms and moved deftly around the room. Tyra motioned for another change, and a Fox Trot came on. The couple danced around the room while Tyra tilted her head. "Tango?" The rhythmic beat of a dramatic Tango began to play, and Tino dipped Jordan before moving abruptly across the floor in a pulsing footwork.

"Well, you have potential," Tyra began once the demonstration was over and Jordan Jensen had moved on her way, successfully flying under Tyra's recognition radar. Tyra Fields had been staring at Tino trying to look bored without much notice of his partner. "You need to move out your steps in your smooth dances — they're a bit choppy. But your Latin has a good feel to it." She stopped and cradling her head in her palms announced, "I guess we could try it. Yeah, ok. I agree. We can try a partnership. I need a week to get myself into shape. So shall we say next Monday?" Then not waiting for an answer she waved him away and turned toward her office. She needed the time to get her mind back into competition mode. That mode was long gone and needed reviving. She put her head down on the desk and closed her eyes. Her first day back had felt good — really good.

Trixie sat at the front desk tapping her eyeglasses on the top of the desk nervously. She picked up the phone and putting her glasses back on, searched the top of the desk for a moment to collect her thoughts. Finally, she dialed and asked for Megan at the downtown studio. She made arrangements to meet the next day for an early lunch at a quaint café in the uptown area.

The patio of the café was empty at ten forty–five in the morning. The Mexican brick on the floor and surrounding wall gave the atmosphere a casual look. Each of the small round tables had a colorful umbrella to shelter from the heat of the sun. Trixie sat at a table on the far side away from any incoming customer traffic. She studied the menu for a few moments before Megan whisked in to join her. Megan had a new hairdo as usual. Her still purple hue was now close cropped on the sides and back with a long heavy bang covering one side of her face. She wore a bright blue suit with a short jacket that sported a ruffled cuff and collar. The calf length skirt was full and soft. Her shoes matched the blue in the suit and had contrasting yellow heels and toe tips. She looked lively yet professional as usual.

"I'll have the chicken and walnut salad with the dressing on the side, please. Make it blue cheese and a large ice tea." Trixie slapped the menu back on the table and waited for Megan to order a wild rice soup in a whole wheat bread bowl and pink lemonade.

"OK, so how was the first day back? I'm sure that's why you needed a lunch meeting – away from the studio. Am I right?" Megan grinned with that knowing Cheshire Cat look on her face.

"It's much worse than you can imagine. Tyra is partnering with Tino."

Megan gasped. She had expected maybe a confrontation with Jordan Jensen or maybe the usual run in with Edward Garrett, but a new partnership? And with Tino Van Arp? This was totally unexpected.

"Why in heaven's name would she do that?" Megan's voice began to squeak.

"He made her an offer she couldn't refuse, I guess. It was his idea and not hers originally, but I think it sparked some things in her mind that she wasn't expecting to feel." Trixie shook her head as the drinks were set down. Megan grabbed the straw of her lemonade and took a deep sip. Trixie only stirred her drink for moment with a faraway look in her eyes.

They both pondered for a few silent minutes thinking through the implications of this partnership. And in a way, they mourned for Cameron Vessi. They mourned for the way it used to be. He was a buffer between Tyra and "the rest". Now Tino would never assume that role. No, it would be a living hell with those two partnering. Not just for the two of them, but for the rest of the studio and the staff. Megan took in the news with anticipated great sadness for the future.

They ate in silence and when the meal ended, Megan gave Trixie a knowing hug and promised she would be a support for the uncertainty that would surely take over the suburban studio. She left her with a convincing "I'll be there for you" speech and a wave of her hand.

Tino and Tyra began practices that Monday with a flourish. Trixie didn't want to be there for the start of it, so took the time to run errands before getting to the studio right around the start of the meeting. Tyra gave her a glower of a look as if to ask why she was so late, but Trixie paid no attention as she set her purse and Target bag behind her chair and looked patiently over the day's schedule. She was sure she would be informed of the progress of the earlier rehearsal some time during the day, and she was.

"I will be so-o-o-o sore tomorrow," whined Tyra when she called Trixie into her office after the meeting ended. "I really thought I had gotten myself into somewhat better shape this past week with some running and exercises, but nothing prepared me for a full out dance rehearsal like the one Tino and I had." She actually glowed as she talked about the anticipated pain. "I will feel it tomorrow!" She leaned back in her chair with a satisfied smirk.

"And I'm sure that stiffness will feel great," Trixie replied in a somewhat bland tone.

"Yes, it will," Tyra didn't notice the unenthusiastic effort in Trixie's voice and mistakenly took her comments to be encouraging. "I'm really looking forward to this partnership. Yes, I am."

Trixie nodded and went over the daily schedule not mentioning Tino Van Arp at all. She had a sinking feeling in the pit of her stomach whenever she thought of this union. And union it would be. It wasn't long before the two were an item. Dating was not really the correct word in a dance studio. There was never any time to actually go out into the world and date like normal people. No movies or dinner dates. No country club or night clubbing. The relationships developed in the studio with everyone around feeling the chemistry between people emerge. The chemistry between Tyra and Tino was steamy. They were both volatile personalities with tempers that could boil over at any moment. It was always clear what had happened at a rehearsal just by the sparks that zipped across the room during the meeting hour. If there were smiles and sly looks, they had had a great rehearsal. But if there were daggers stinging across the room, it hadn't gone well at all. It was a soap opera without words.

It was on that Friday when Trixie came in early that she was caught in a surprise. She slid into her chair noiselessly and was bending down to slip into her dance shoes when she heard the yelling and then the thud. Shaking, she lowered even more. Then carefully peeking over the top of the desk, she saw Tino bodily throw Tyra into the wall. Tyra slid down the wall with a whimper clutching her back. Tino stopped yelling and stomped out past the front desk to the hallway. Tyra carefully picked herself up and retreated to her office.

It wasn't that Trixie thought Tyra wasn't an active participant in the fight. She was certain Tyra had been right in the thick of the whole thing probably provoking the wrath of Tino Van Arp. But to see her like this was heartbreaking and violent.

Trixie sighed. Straightening up, she stood and moved toward the door of the office. Tyra was on the phone. "Yes, I would like to report an attack. Yes, that's right. I was assaulted by my boyfriend."

Tyra had reported Tino to the police. They would be coming soon to take a statement and talk with Tino about the incident. Before they arrived, Trixie had an opportunity to talk with Tyra.

"Just what went on here?" Trixie asked without a demanding tone, but with no sympathy either.

"Tino attacked me. He shoved me into the wall. You can see the bruise here on my back and on my arms where he grabbed me," she flung out her bare arms. Still dressed in her workout t-shirt and leggings, she raised her shirt to show the beginning stages of a bruise.

"What happened before he did this?" Trixie folded her arms and waited.

"He's done this before, you know." Tyra continued on ignoring Trixie's question about the incident. "He's hit me. I've even had a black eye. But I covered it with make-up so no one would know. Not even you."

"What were you arguing about? Why are you ignoring my question?" Trixie persisted not letting her change the subject.

"He's not a good dancer," Tyra continued in a whinny voice. "He's so not Cameron. I can't stand his attitude. He doesn't want me to help him at all with his poor, shoddy technique. Why not? Why is he so belligerent when I'm only trying to make him better — make our partnership better. I'm just so much **better** than he is…" Tyra was no longer the suffering victim but the angry superior professional who was more than willing to put down someone's abilities in no uncertain terms. She didn't care how she said it — if it was truth, it had to be blunt. That was her philosophy with dance. Tell it like it is. Make them feel the pain.

The police arrived. They interviewed Tyra Fields, and she certainly showed them her scars. Then they took Tino Van Arp into custody and walked him out the door as the rest of the staff was arriving. Heads turned in stunned curiosity, and the whispers were evident the entire day. Of course, Tino was released when Tyra decided not to press charges. "I only wanted to scare him," she later confessed to Edward Garrett as he tapped his foot impatiently when he ordered Trixie to find a new teacher to teach Tino's evening lessons. "He'll be back tomorrow," Tyra explained coyly to Trixie as she picked up the phone to make her calls. "There aren't really any bruises to show for it. I guess my skin is just sensitive. Just a little redness that's already gone away." She looked around pursing her lips at Edward's piercing eyes. "I may have hit him first..." That was Tino's story, and it seemed to be true after all.

The rehearsals continued, and the fighting as well. But there weren't any more charges made — just yelling and once a broken window in the door between the small and large studio. Evidently "someone" threw a shoe or a shoe brush through the window during a rehearsal. It shattered and had to be replaced before the students arrived. Trixie was not happy with her new role as "fixer".

After a few months, Tyra and Tino were preparing for the Las Vegas competition and decided a dress rehearsal was necessary. So at the weekly studio party, they asked to be the performance routine showcased. Edward Garrett and the rest of the staff were curious to see the results of this new partnership. Would it measure up to the partnership Tyra Fields had with Cameron Vessi? No one expected anywhere near the same intensity those two had, but they were wrong.

When the music began, Tyra entered in a stunning Latin dress made of see-through lace. It was long with a slit up the side and the flesh colored body suit she wore underneath gave the illusion of a naked body covered with a sheer layer of lace. Her platinum blond hair was pulled up into a knot on top of her head and twined with a string of sparkling stones. Her vibrant make-up was stunning with an accent of crystal stone glued to her cheek and eyebrow. She wore high flesh toned dance shoes — strappy and delicate that made her legs look miles long. Tino wore a white opened neck Latin shirt that matched the creamy color of Tyra's lace. His black dance pants emphasized his lean body and thin, strong legs. Although taller than Tyra, his Latin dance shoes sported a higher Cuban heel that gave him a few extra inches to tower over her piled high hair style.

They began with a Cha Cha — rhythmic and sharp with tight movements of the legs and feet. Tino turned Tyra sharply hitting each pose with dramatic flair. Crisp movement across the floor in locking positions with the feet then into swivels and spins gave the cheering crowd moments of excitement. Tyra gazed into the audience, made eye contact with someone and winked. Just as quickly, they moved into a Swing with softened bounces and fast moving feet kicking and twirling across the floor. They flashed smiles at the crowd as they playfully felt the beat of the music. Suddenly the music slowed into a romantic Rumba, and they seemed intensely interested in gazing into each others' eyes with hands caressing the face and body not only of each other but of themselves. Tyra gently stroked her own face and down her neck as she turned to move away from Tino, then she swiveled back and jutting her chin forward toward his face, she wrapped up into his arms and suddenly dropped to the floor. The viewers erupted in wild applause.

They held the dropped pose for a moment and then helping his partner to her feet, Tino spread his arms in reception of the applause. He spun Tyra in front of him, and she bowed gracefully. They had succeeded in winning over the audience. They were indeed ready for Las Vegas.

As they exited the floor, Tyra whispered breathlessly to Tino, "That went quite well, I think. Now we just have to make sure our smooth dances are as clean as our rhythm. We'll be OK then." She sucked in a deep breath. He nodded looking over his shoulder to see whose eyes followed his exit out. He smiled.

X.

That is how Tyra Fields found herself on the plane to Las Vegas. She tried to relax, but the plane was experiencing some turbulence. She couldn't sleep as she had planned. Tomorrow was going to be her comeback. She would show the dance world that she, Tyra Fields, was indeed a champion — even without Cameron Vessi. Yes, she missed him. She saw him every day in the eyes of her daughter. He was someone she wouldn't – couldn't – forget. But now was a new chapter in her life. Now she was going to show the world Tyra Fields was good — no, not just good, but the best. She fidgeted in her seat and glanced again down the aisle at Tino. How could he sleep at a time like this? But there he was. Stretched out with eyes tightly closed, he was so relaxed and comfortable it made her angry. She wanted to throw a shoe at him and wake him up so he could be as uncomfortable as she was. Her elbow shoved a little on the man in the seat next to hers in an attempt to move him back into his space. He grunted, and she groaned.

Finally the flight attendant announced their arrival in Las Vegas. She could hear the wheels lowering and the plane hit the pavement of the runway. It bounced a bit and then slid to a slow grinding stop. But before anyone could rise from their seat, there was another announcement to "remain seated". Curiously, Tyra looked around as two policemen scurried in through the opened door and stopped suddenly at Tino Van Arp's seat. They motioned for him to get up and then slipped a pair of handcuffs around his wrists. He looked dazed and confused glancing back to catch Tyra's eye.

When the rest of the passengers were allowed to disembark, Tyra Fields quickly looked around the terminal for Edward Garrett. Grabbing him as he waited for his luggage to circle, she gripped his arm and gritting her teeth snarled, "Do something!"

He looked curiously at her as she explained that Tino Van Arp had been dragged off the plane in handcuffs. "He is not going to ruin my debut at this competition. Find him and get him released!" she demanded.

Edward quickly snatched his bag and hurried toward the exit to find out what had happened. Tyra's face was pinched and angry. What had he done? What was happening?

She caught the shuttle to the hotel. When the bellhop tried to help her with her luggage, she snatched the bags away and dragging them to the desk checked in. "If you could direct any messages to me immediately…" she begged the clerk at the desk. "I'm expecting an urgent call. Thanks." And she tried to put on a half way acceptable smile as the clerk nodded without meeting her wide eyed stare.

Tyra unpacked and lay on her bed. She gazed at the ceiling. Her eyes tried to close for a much needed nap, but she was worried. Just as she was about to doze off, a sharp wrap on the door made her jump with a start. She opened the door and stared at Edward Garrett gripping the shirt of a squirming Tino Van Arp. They slid in, and Edward released his grip. "OK, tell her what this is all about," he demanded.

Tino's eyelids were half closed as if he had been just awakened from a deep sleep. "They found a joint in my luggage." His voice was soft with a 'no big deal' whine.

"What!" she answered as if she hadn't heard him — which quite possibly had been the case as his voice was so low.

"They found a joint in my luggage," he repeated this time a little louder and firmer.

"How could you? How could you do something like this when you know how important this is to me?" her voice shrilled to a high pitched shriek.

"You? You? Why is it always about YOU?" Tino's voice was no longer soft but began to boom. He walked across the room and collapsed on the bed. "I have trouble on planes and needed to relax a bit. Lay off!"

"I paid his bail. He has to be arraigned before we leave for home, but luckily I got it scheduled for after the competition dancing ends so that won't be interrupted." Edward could come through when the chips were down. "He'll plead guilty and pay a fine hopefully. First offense and all."

"Thanks. Thanks for that, I guess," Tyra frowned and tried to take in the information. It didn't do any good to get angrier when their dancing depended on a good relationship between the two of them. "Let's try to keep this quiet, shall we?"

91

"I think that would be best," Edward agreed. "Now can I expect that he will be here in your room? He has a room booked, but I think it best if we quietly keep him here where you can keep an eye on him. Don't let anyone know where he is. He's made a spectacle of himself already. Lay low!" he ordered pointing at Tino with a snarl.

Tyra nodded. She didn't look forward to sneaking around with Tino sharing her room, but she knew it was for the best. She sighed and flopped down on the bed to collect her thoughts as Edward Garrett moved to leave. "I'll check him in downstairs, but you stay with him twenty–four seven. Got it?" She nodded and buried her head in her hands. What a great time this was going to be!

After a boring hour of watching Tino snore, she decided to tour the hotel and see what was what. The hallway was empty except for a suitcase she recognized to be the bag Tino had brought to the airport. It was standing alone next to a door down to the right. She snatched the bag, dragged it to her door and quickly stored it in the closet with the sliding doors just inside the entry of her room. No need to advertise his presence to the cleaning staff. Then she proceeded down the hall to the elevator.

The hotel was lovely as all hotels in Las Vegas seem to be. Glittery and colorful, they attempted to draw in the tourist with all there is to try — shops, casinos, and mouthwatering food. Tyra wasn't hungry, so she ambled along to take a look at the ballroom where she would be performing. Best to scope out the floor well ahead of time. She followed the signs. This hotel was filled with dancers for the big event. It would last several days not only featuring the best professional dancers in the country but also a wide variety of pro-am competitors. Pro-am divisions were divided into both male and female amateurs dancing with their professional teachers. They included young children up to the elderly. Each competitor was divided by age and sex into competitive groups. The official time schedule for each competing group was printed on large signs and displayed in front of the ballroom area. Tyra checked through the long list to find who would be in their original heats. She and Tino were in both the smooth and rhythm divisions in American style. Many couples chose either one or the other but not both. She and Tino were the exception to the rule.

Scanning the lists, she scoped out the competition. Only the top dancers in each heat would move on to the semi-finals and then on to the finals. It was a grueling competition day as each dancer tried to dance full out for each level. By the finals, each competitor had already put out every ounce of energy in the previous heats just to get there to the final. They would need every bit of stamina to get through to the end. Tyra checked out the size of the floor and stepped on the wood slats to check how slippery the finish felt. It was uncomfortable to have a surface that was too slick. There were other couples out on the floor warming up their routines to check for spacing. The judges would be positioned around the floor, and each couple would try to imagine where they would want certain combinations placed for best visibility by a judge.

Tyra meandered out the double doors to the large area reserved for the venders. These competitions were the best places for dance merchandise to be displayed and purchased. Everything imaginable was carefully placed for maximum attraction. There were booths of dance shoes, jewelry, hairpieces, music, and costumes. Tyra noticed a few favorite brands and moved on past the beaded purses and glittery face make-up toward the dance attire.

"Wow! This is a fabulous dress," she commented as she fingered a ball gown in silky deep lavender with a deep front v neckline and stoning on the bodice. She looked around for a vender name on the booth and was surprised to spot a "Gowns by Karen" sign. Karen Danbury was here in Las Vegas and displayed a stunning line of dresses. Her line was very innovative and distinct. Tyra entered the booth and looked through the books displaying more of Karen's designs.

Most professional dancers preferred to match the male and female dancers' costumes, then keeping that color scheme for the year will sell back the used costume to the vendor and purchase a new design for the next year. That way, they looked fresh each season. The newer dancers were always eager to pick up a used matching costume for much less money than a new design would cost. The dance dresses were especially pricy, costing thousands of dollars new. A used dress would cost upwards of a thousand or two. That way the vendor would recycle the costumes, make a little money on the old ones and always insure a sale of a new set designed specially to new trends — updated and unique. The styles change year to year.

Tyra decided she should begin selection of next year's dresses soon. It always took a while to select the color, fabric and design much less take the time out of rehearsals for fittings. Karen was certainly making her name in the costume design business. These photos and samples were stunning.

Karen was helping an older dancer select a style for a smooth dance dress. Tyra caught her eye and fluttered her red polished nails in her direction. Karen blinked and then with a startled realization on her face waved back. She excused herself and moved in Tyra's direction.

"I didn't expect to see you here in Las Vegas!" she greeted with a catch in her voice and a raise of one eyebrow.

"Yes, I'm partnering with Tino Van Arp these days. You remember Tino?" Tyra looked past Karen's plain face toward a vibrant yellow gown hanging on display.

"Yes, yes of course. I remember Tino," Karen's face showed a bit of a frown. "I just heard about Cameron. One of the judges mentioned they attended his funeral. I am so sorry."

"Over and done with, my dear. I am on to a new and better partner now. No sense worrying about the past. Spilled milk…water under the bridge, and such." She snatched a corner of the yellow skirt and slid the fabric through her fingers. "My, this is lovely. What do you expect for next year? What trends do you anticipate?"

Karen's face pinched into an angry sour expression. "I think maybe this is too soon…" she began.

"Do you think a lower neckline would be good for a smooth dress? I have a blue color in mind with a light blue on the top and then gradually moving through the shades to a navy at the bottom of the skirt. What do you think about that idea?" Tyra didn't notice the startled shock in Karen's eyes and continued to ramble on about her next dress design. "Where are you located these days?"

"I'm working out of a studio here in Las Vegas during the summer months and have a place in Florida during the winter," Karen answered with a crisp edge to her tone.

"Perfect. Then I could order and do a few fittings here. Fly out for a weekend…" Tyra's voice trailed off. Just as her head snapped toward

96

another dress hanging next to the yellow number, an elderly white haired lady approached and grabbed Tyra's elbow.

"Tyra Fields! What a surprise! I'm so sorry to hear about poor Cameron. He was such a dear." Mrs. Watson, a long time amateur competitor with an ear for gossip closed in on Tyra.

Tyra smiled and carried on a rather lengthy conversation about Cameron Vessi, his dancing accomplishments, illness, and death. Karen Danbury slipped by to help a group of customers crowded around a shimmering white dress on display by the cash register.

Next stop, the jewelry booths. Tyra made a point to pick up some of her most stunning dance jewelry at these competitions. It was important to shine when dancing out on the floor — anything to make the crowd and judges look in your direction. She fingered a few pieces and finally selected a pair of large sparkly earrings that would work well with her smooth dress.

She saw a few other dancers from her past and repeated the Cameron Vessi story more than she cared to. Finally, it was too much to take and she moved to a part of the hotel not so populated by dancers to find a quiet area to call Trixie. Best not wait any longer to let her know what had happened on the plane to Vegas. She was sure Edward hadn't bothered to call back a report.

The call was relatively short. Trixie Appleby was initially shocked by Tino's arrest and appropriately soothing in her assurance that "things would work out". "We'll be dancing later this afternoon and tonight. So I suppose I should get my energy up by eating a little something. Don't want to run out of steam in the finals!" Tyra set her sights high and signed off with a bit of optimism that made Trixie chuckle.

"Let me know what happens. I'll expect a call right after it ends tonight," she replied. "Promise me."

"I will," Tyra agreed looking toward the list of food options the hotel offered. Should she order into the room? No. Eating with Tino snoring away in the corner would be irritating. Find a nice patio and get a little fresh air and sun. So she did.

XI.

Smooth dances first. They stood ready to go on. The tension was thick — each couple wanting a nod to go on to the next level. Each one pacing, stretching out, prancing in their dance shoes to ready for the trip out to the floor. Tyra and Tino were no different than the rest. They walked around lightly stepping through a few steps, taking a few deep breathes. Pace. Pace. Pace. Shake off any nerves.

98

Finally, their heat was called. They waited for their names to be announced and scampered out to the floor with a quick turn and plastered toothy smiles toward the crowd. Finding a spot on the floor in front of a stony faced judge, Tyra and Tino smiled at each other and waited for the music to begin. They would start with the Waltz then move to Tango, Fox Trot and finally the Viennese Waltz.

Tyra's gown shimmered as she spun into her Waltz entrance holding her dance pose as Tino swayed into position to twinkle around the line of dance. Swinging his body into a pendulum motion, Tino glided across the floor and began a pivot right in front of judge number two. Into the next corner Tyra swung her leg into a ronde and leaned back into an X line. The Waltz continued strong. The music ended, and the audience clapped as the couples regrouped to begin the Tango.

The music was pulsing and dramatic. Tino moved quickly, his flat dance shoes caressing the floor with each movement. Then he led a series of quick flares for Tyra and once again a pivot into a high kick and ronde. They looked smart and sharp at each quick change. One judge raised an eyebrow as they began a few foot changes. Tino worked hard to maintain a somber facial expression when he so wanted to cheer for that last movement. It was well done.

Fox Trot was a change of pace. Regaining a smile and a head toss to the Broadway style music, Tino's body moved easily and gracefully around the floor. Tyra's ribcage stretched side extending a "come hither" hand toward a corner judge. Just as quickly, Tino pulled her back and they twirled around the floor with a controlled and relaxed footwork that gave lightness to their movement. Tyra's closed toed smooth dance shoes were dyed to match her dress. The satiny finish glistened in the spot lights as did the stone work on her bodice. A flip of her skirt billowed and surrounded her legs like a soft cloud of green. Tyra knew this was their best smooth dance, and she flashed a knowing smile as they passed another judge, craning his head to watch them pass.

The final dance, the Viennese Waltz was a fast, spinning blur. They wound around the floor, skirt swirling behind as they clutched tightly in a closed dance position until the very end when Tino rolled Tyra out and just as quickly spun her back in to a long lunging extension. The crowd was on its feet in applause. Tino raised his arms in acknowledgement as did Tyra then bowed into a low curtsy. The applause continued as the couples twirled off the floor.

Tino and Tyra were called back to the semi-finals in the smooth dance category and repeated their performance. However, they didn't make it past the semis and retreated to the sidelines to pout. Edward rushed up and congratulated them even if they didn't make the finals.

"That was a superb performance," he bellowed giving Tyra a quick hug and patting Tino on the back. "Now get back into that game and put on your Latin attitude. You've got this. You've got this," he repeated over and over again.

They didn't stop to watch the finals. It was on to the next challenge. Changing quickly into their rhythm attire, Tyra took the time to reposition her long platinum locks. Many of the dancers she had competed against before didn't recognize her with her new hair color. They were so used to seeing her with the dark hair that this slender blond woman didn't register in their minds as Tyra Fields. That was just fine with Tyra. This was a new start — a new beginning as a different person. She chuckled when some stared too long trying to remember where they had seen her before. She liked being "unknown".

The creamy lace dress was unusual and stood out from the other women in their heat. Most dresses were short and glittery. The long length and hint of nudity turned heads as Tino and Tyra bounded out to the dance floor when the announcer called their names. Position. Wait – wait – wait. Listen for the music. Start. Their Cha Cha was a show stopper. The Rumba was sexy and electric. Swing fast and flirty, and their Bolero sensual and exciting.

Last on the agenda was the fast and ever challenging Mambo. Tino loved the Mambo. He had a Latin style that couldn't be beat, and his Mambo was especially dynamic. There was a special little kick he put into his steps that gave it added flare. The judges from all parts of the floor gravitated toward Tino and his Mambo. Their heads rotated to watch. With his dark Latin look, he was someone who stood apart from the others. This was his dance, and he knew it.

They once again made the semi-finals. But this time, when the semis were over, they were at the top. They were chosen for the finals in the rhythm dances. Sucking in air and shaking out their hands and feet. They needed a little added push to do the dances just one more time. Try to kick it up a notch — make it past the other dancers who were also trying to pump up their game as well.

Edward Garrett gave them a thumbs up from the edge of the crowd and smiled his famous chipmunk grin. He was dressed in a well tailored cream colored suit with a splash of color in a pale blue dress shirt with a skinny white tie and cream colored dance shoes. His head of curly hair — a toupee that no one dared comment on in his presence — was patted into place, and he had a long silk scarf draped over his shoulders that reached past the bottom of his jacket hem. Clinging to his arm was a tall slender redhead with a clingy dress that seemed barely on her body. Another of Edward's bimbos, sighed Tyra as she glanced quickly to nod at the thumbs up. She smiled. When would he ever learn?

The tension mounted as the couples positioned along the edges of the dance floor tried to stand calmly but rocked back and forth with nervous energy. The announcer called out the placements – last to first.

Tyra and Tino were called to the floor in second place. As they accepted the congratulations from the judge and a medal, Tino grumbled under his breath. "Save it," Tyra ordered through a clenched smile. "The first place couple would have won even if they did only basics around that floor. Their reputation puts them in first place automatically. They're that good." She grabbed and pumped the hand of the next judge who moved from couple to couple with a few words and a smile.

Off the floor, Tyra sat in an uncharacteristic sprawl. She was tired. Bending down to unbuckle her shoes, she heard Mrs. Crawford scurry up to greet Tino with a hug and congratulations. Mrs. Crawford was an elderly woman with blue hair piled on her head who had been a regular student of Cameron's. At this competition, Tino would dance with her in the pro-am division. She would probably do quite well considering her age group. Tyra crouched down even more trying to be invisible. She just wasn't in the mood to have any type of conversation with Mrs. Crawford.

"You did so well Mr. Van Arp, but I'm sure you would certainly have won with another partner. That blond woman doesn't have the personality on the floor that Jordan Jensen has. She and Mr. Vessi made such a cute couple. If only you would have been able to dance today with Miss Jensen, surely you would have won," Mrs. Crawford babbled on and on. Then left a red faced Tino Van Arp standing alone and embarrassed. He felt the glare of eyes to his back.

103

Tyra stood abruptly and faced her partner. "Follow me, please," she said with a plastered smile that dipped a bit too much on the ends. He followed her toward the restroom area which was now empty and void of crowds.

She suddenly turned to face him nose to nose. Then she snarled, "So what is this about that little tramp I caught with my husband being back in the studio?"

"Jordan? Jordan Jensen?" Tino stammered. "Mr. Garrett hired her back when you left on maternity leave. She's in the suburban studio. The little dark haired one…"

Wham! Tyra's right hand came across his face hard. Tino quickly touched the painful cheek and frowned. "It has nothing to do with me!" Wham! She hit him with the left hand across the other cheek.

Tino didn't even have the time to protect himself as her fists began to randomly pummel him across the head, arms and shoulders. "Traitor!" she screamed with a growl in her voice. "Why didn't you tell me?"

Just as quickly as the blows began, they ended. Two uniformed officers were holding Tyra Fields arms. "Are you all right, sir?" one of them asked as Tino shook his head in disbelief. "Do you need a medic?"

They led the two of them to a small back security office and settling an angry Tyra on a long wooden bench, handcuffed her hand to the arm of the seat. Pointing an accusing finger in her direction, one of the officers ordered her to "stay put". Then they got an ice pack for Tino and put him on the other side of the room. The clock ticked off slowly with no one coming to even speak to Tyra. She sat uncomfortably for a long time and then sprawled out on the bench and closed her eyes to wait. The one officer remaining in the station sat behind a tall desk and refused to make eye contact with either Tyra or Tino. A few times the phone rang or a walkie talkie crackled, but Tyra didn't pay much attention. Her thoughts were on Jordan Jensen. How had she missed the woman? Why hadn't she recognized her? It was the fact that no one consulted with her on the matter or even mentioned her presence that really began to eat at her brain. How could Edward Garrett betray her like that?

Suddenly the phone calls began to stir some activity. She heard the officer request back up for a room on the fifth floor. It had been hours that she had been on this bench. Looking up at the clock, she realized she had fallen asleep, and it was now the middle of the night. The conversation began to squawk from the walkie talkie – "man down. Request ambulance. Request assistance!" The words were fading in and out. Something was going on that was obviously more important than her little incident with Tino. People rushed in and out with a few more calls coming in, and the officer behind the desk showing more and more alarm in his "huhs" and "yups".

After what seemed to be a lifetime, an officer un-cuffed Tyra from the bench and motioned her into a small room. She sat at the table with an officer across from her.

"We have a situation here…" he began clearing his throat.

"Yes, I know. I lost my temper and…" she tried to explain her reaction.

"No, Miss Fields. Not that situation. We have a murder. Edward Garrett was murdered tonight in his hotel room." He waited for her reaction.

Tyra's face flushed and her eyes grew larger. "Oh my goodness. Oh my goodness." She sat back and clutched her chest blinking her eyes. She was wide awake now.

"Do you know anyone who would want to murder Mr. Garrett," the officer sat pen poised over a blank notebook.

Tyra laughed a nervous twitter. "If we were in Minneapolis, I could tell you lots of people who would like to see Mr. Garrett dead. But we're in Las Vegas. That's a different story. Of course, he knows lots of people with the dance competition here and all, but I suppose he could have made some enemies in the past that I wouldn't know about. He's a complicated man who is either loved or hated. He tends to attract strong emotions on either end of the spectrum." She frowned in an attempt to think. Who would have killed Edward?

"We have another little twist to this whole situation," the officer continued clicking his pen nervously. "He may have been murdered to set you up for that murder."

Tyra's mouth fell opened, and she stared into his eye for the first time.

"As soon as we found the body, we received an anonymous call from someone who said the murder weapon was in your hotel room. And indeed we found the knife that appears to have stabbed him in your bathroom wastebasket." He let those words sink in before he continued. "Luckily for you, I guess, you had this little incident with Mr. Van Arp because you were handcuffed to our bench during the time of the murder. So that weapon was planted by someone who didn't know you had an air tight alibi."

This time Tyra was in shock. "So now I need to ask you, who would want to harm you? Do you have any enemies here in Vegas?" His voice was steady and calm.

Tyra's lips twisted nervously. This was particularly unsettling. Who would want to put her in this position? Who would want to frame her for murder?

XII.

Tyra placed a call to Trixie Appleby as soon as she was allowed.
"Are you sitting down?" she began.

Trixie chuckled. "I'm always sitting down. What's up?"

"Edward Garrett has been murdered."

There was a long silence. Then Tyra explained what she knew
about the situation. She told her about the second place finish, the
overheard conversation between Tino and Mrs. Crawford, the fight and the
night in the security office. Then she went on. "Someone placed the
murder weapon in my hotel room and called in a tip to the police."

"Wow! I don't know if I'm seated low enough for all of this. So I
assume Tino also has an air tight alibi as well?" Trixie interjected.

Tyra hadn't thought that far. But she supposed Tino was ruled out
as a suspect as well. He wasn't the enemy she would have to worry about.
Maybe that was good — comforting to have someone she could trust. She
realized she was shaking. "What should I do, Trixie? I'm sure we will
have to stay here longer if things are not settled soon."

Trixie pondered. Then she responded. "I'm pretty sure the
murderer would have to be connected to the competition. Otherwise why
try to steer the blame to you. The murderer must know both of you. So I

want you to fax me copies of the program with everyone who is listed in attendance — judges, dancers, vendors. Anyone who is there. I am going to call the coordinators and see if they can get me a more complete list, but you fax me that program ASAP. Got that? I'm going to check through names and do a bit of research on those attending. That's the best we can do from here." Trixie tapped her pen on the top of the desk and scribbled a few notes. "Got to go. Keep me updated on anything — and I mean anything — that happens."

An hour later Trixie was scanning the sheets Tyra had faxed to her. Her glasses perched on her nose gave her an intense look as she frowned at a few of the names. She highlighted some with a yellow marker and pondered what to do next.

Tyra Fields sat at a small round table with a plate of pancakes and a large mug of steaming coffee. She was grateful for this time alone so she could scan the headlines in the paper and find out what the police had neglected to inform her about last night's murder. Evidently Edward Garrett was found in his room stabbed to death by a hotel cocktail waitress. Tyra assumed she was the redhead Edward had displayed prominently on his arm during the evening's competition. The waitress had to work a shift and was to meet him after work. He had given her a keycard to his room and when she entered found him splayed across the bed with a good deal of blood surrounding the body. She had called security immediately. They determined he had been dead for several hours. There was mention of finding the murder weapon, but where and how was not in the article. Tyra wondered if the person who had planted the knife in her room would be waiting for her arrest. "Hmmm." She gulped her coffee and dropped the paper to the table. Then slapping a few dollars on the table top, she put her head down and headed to the security office —by now she knew the way with no hesitation.

"I think you need to arrest me," she stated flatly as she rested her arms on the tall desk in the corner.

The officer behind the desk looked at her curiously. He was newly on shift and did not know who this woman with the strange request might be. She explained to him the problems she had last night, and he nodded knowingly. Evidently he was familiar with the report but not with exactly with who she was. "If someone planted the murder weapon in my room, they are going to expect you to arrest me for the murder. And if you don't, I'm going to be in danger!" Tyra's voice rose a pitch higher.

The officer got on the phone and called a supervisor. Tyra waited on the same bench she had occupied for the entire night. It seemed to form fit to her seated body way too neatly. Then she repeated her story over again for the supervisor. "In order to catch the real murderer, you need to let them think I am arrested for the murder. Don't you see that?" Tyra began to shake again pleading her case.

They decided to hold a press conference that morning to announce an arrest for the murder, and in the mean time, Tyra would be secluded in a new room under another name. She wasn't to tell anyone except Trixie about the plan. Even Tino would be kept in the dark about Tyra's whereabouts. Tyra had to wonder how the murderer had gotten into her room. Had Tino slipped his keycard to someone? At that thought, she snatched up her bag and began to paw through it to find her keycard. Hmmm. Missing! Someone was close enough to her bag to steal her key. And it would have to be someone who would recognize her bag — maybe during the competition when she was out on the floor. Who could wander through the back rooms used for changing during a competition and not be noticed? That would narrow down the suspects.

Tyra made a call to Trixie to tell her about the plan. She wanted her to know before the announcement could be made about the arrest of a suspect. She also wanted her to know about the missing keycard. That would narrow Trixie's search for a plausible suspect.

Trixie did indeed find this last bit of information interesting. That certainly seemed to point to a dance competition attendee. Of course, a hotel employee could wander through the back rooms carrying a pitcher of water or table ... was that likely? Maybe she would have to contact the hotel about an employee list as well. But then again, an employee would have access to a master keycard and wouldn't need to steal Tyra's. A list would be helpful, and she was curious to see if a familiar name popped up.

The TVs in the lobby interrupted with the press conference. When the announcement was made about the suspect already in custody, Tino gasped. He was standing next to Mrs. Crawford preparing to practice on the dance floor when his eye caught the news brief. He hadn't seen Tyra Fields for hours. He had assumed she was sleeping, but when he went back to the room earlier, it was empty. At the time, he didn't think anything of it, but now. Could they have arrested Tyra for the murder? It seemed impossible, but now his brain was going quickly over the facts he knew. She certainly hadn't left the security office last night during the time the murder was committed. Had she had an accomplice? Is that why she had started the fight? To give herself an alibi? His mind was working overtime now. Had she shared her room with him to cast suspicion on someone else — him? There were so many possibilities. His thoughts were interrupted by the chatter of Mrs. Crawford.

"I'm ready, dear. I am so glad they have the murderer in custody. That is such a relief. Shall we get out on that floor and give it a go?" Mrs. Crawford patted her hair into place and flashed Tino a cheerful smile. He followed her to the edge of the floor and scanned the square for an open area to practice. The floor was packed with dancers.

XIII.

Trixie hung up the phone and pondered this latest development. She stared down at her notes and sighed. This certainly wasn't going to work. She was going to have to get on a plane and go to Las Vegas. That was the only solution to solving this crisis – both for Tyra Fields and for Edward Garrett.

Ashley Arthur pranced into the studio earlier than the rest of the staff and greeted Trixie cheerfully just as she rose from her chair, pushed her paperwork into her large hand bag and swung around the corner of the reception desk.

"I'm on my way to Las Vegas," she announced hurriedly explaining. "Take over while I'm gone!"

Ashley dropped his jaw and in a stutter asked if she had a ticket. "Do you have a ride to the airport? When is the next flight leaving?"

"Call a taxi for me, would you?" She hoisted her hand bag to her shoulder and headed for the door."Oh, by the way…Edward Garrett was murdered!" Without even waiting for Ashley's reaction to this announcement, she headed for the end of the corridor to the ATM machine for a little travel cash and waited outside for the yellow cab to pull up to the curb. While she waited, she pulled out her phone and called Tyra to let her know of her new plans. "When I get to the hotel, I'll call. You can direct me to your room. Ta ta!" She hung up and slid into the back of the cab.

Trixie didn't have long to wait for a flight out and caught another taxi to the hotel housing the dance competition. The lobby was elegant and sparkly. She found an overstuffed chair and settled in before calling Tyra. It had been a long trip in a very short time.

"Ok, I'm in the lobby of the hotel. Where should I go?" Trixie listened carefully. Her eyes glanced to the left where a row of elevators were taking people in glittery dance gowns up and down. She walked slowly past the crowd to the hallway curving around to the left and came face to face with a locked fire door. Softly she rapped on the metal, and Tyra Fields opened the door. Without speaking to each other, Trixie followed Tyra down the hall past several opened doors with ladders and paint cans inside to a closed door at the end of the corridor. Once inside Tyra spoke.

"Trixie! Why did you come to Las Vegas?" Tyra hugged her before settling back onto the bed. Trixie plopped down into the chair facing the bed and slipped off her shoes.

"You are stuck in this room and unable to defend yourself properly. I certainly can't do much back in Minneapolis. All I could do there was stare at pages of names. Here I can move with the crowds and listen to what people are saying because someone here knows what happened. So tell me your story. Start at the beginning." Trixie demanded as she set her purse down on the floor pulling out the sheets of names.

Tyra began with the flight to Las Vegas, Tino's arrest and rescue by Edward Garrett, and the decision to have Tino stay in her room during the competition. She repeated the conversation between Mrs. Crawford and Tino that led to the fight and arrest. Then she related the shock of Edward's murder, and the tip that led police to the murder weapon in Tyra's room.

"So someone set me up," Tyra's voice shook. "Someone murdered Edward Garrett and set me up to take the fall."

"Well, either you or Tino," Trixie pursed her lips. "Did anyone know Tino was staying in your room?"

"Not that I'm aware of," Tyra stammered. "I didn't tell anyone. I don't know if Tino said something to someone." She paused. "You think someone set up Tino?"

Trixie shrugged her shoulders. "One of you. That is if someone knew Tino was in your room. Who did you say found the body?"

"A woman who works in the hotel. I think she's a waitress in the restaurant. I saw the two of them together during the competition. Evidently she had a late work schedule, and Edward gave her a key card to come to his room after her shift ended. Typical!" Tyra shook her head and rolled her eyes.

"Name?"

"You'll have to check with the police on that. I called the officer I have been dealing with on this matter and told him you were flying in to help. At first he wasn't very pleased, but I explained you could move among the dancers and get information and gossip the police would be unable to get. So then he was very receptive to that idea." Tyra added, "I think you should stay in Tino's original room. No one is in there. We've paid for the room. I see you packed light . . ."

Trixie grabbed her purse and laughed. "I guess this skirt and top are inappropriate attire for the competition."

"Luckily Karen Danbury has a booth set up with lots of dance dresses for sale including a few used costumes at a cheaper price. You might try to pick up a dress from her. She may even give you a discount." Tyra grinned at Trixie Appleby imagining her in a sparkly floating dance gown.

Trixie picked up her notebook and began to make a list. 1. Meet with the police and get a few more details and names. 2. Contact Tino and get the key card for his room. 3. Find Karen and buy a few necessities. 4. Interview the woman who found Edward's body.

"So who do you think is a prime suspect for this murder?" Trixie sat with pen poised ready to put down a number 5.

"Well, I have my suspicions about Mrs. Crawford. She said some pretty nasty things about me when I eavesdropped on her conversation with Tino."

"Little old Mrs. Crawford? She seems to be a long shot." Trixie frowned at the thought of blue haired Mrs. Crawford grabbing a knife and stabbing Edward. "Who else?"

"There is one of the judges who really seems to have something against me. He marks me down at every competition for anything and everything." Trixie looked down at her list of dance judges. "Carl Friend. Tino and I call him Carl the Fiend because he gives us such low scores."

"Carl Friend from Tampa Bay?" Trixie circled the name on her list.

"You know him?"

"A dear, dear friend," Trixie smiled and let out a quick laugh. "Really, we've been friends for a long time. I'll get to the bottom of this scoring problem for you."

Half an hour later Trixie sat in the office of the hotel security with the policeman who was heading the murder investigation. At first he seemed to bristle when she arrived, but as they began to talk, he softened recognizing the help Trixie Appleby could be to his case.

"So I'm undercover?" she asked tilting her head back with a coy smile. The wrinkles around her eyes crinkled with excitement.

"Absolutely!" he chuckled. "So what do you need to know to bring you up to speed on this investigation. I'm sure Tyra Fields has given you most of the information."

"What is the name of the woman who found Edward?" She once again sat poised with pen and notebook in hand. Her memory wasn't what it used to be

"Stephanie Sweet. She works in the restaurant as a waitress. She found Edward around 2:00 AM when she had finished her evening shift. He gave her a keycard to his room earlier and invited her back to his room after she finished work. He was lying on the bed with a stab wound to the heart from a steak knife. There was a serving cart with a steak dinner ordered from room service in front of the bed. The knife was missing but someone called in a tip to our office saying it could be found in room 232 – Tyra Field's room. And when we searched, it was in the bathroom wastebasket covered in Edward Garrett's blood." He had the report opened in front of him reviewing it periodically as he gave Trixie the information.

She wrote down the name "Stephanie Sweet" with a little heart after it. It sounded more like a hooker's name. She wondered if it was her real name or not. "So who called in the tip? And did they mention Tyra's name directly?"

"We don't know but assumed it might be housekeeping. No one has admitted to the call, but they probably don't want to get into trouble," he said shrugging his shoulders. "We know for sure Tyra is innocent because at the time of the murder she was in our custody handcuffed to the bench in our security office." He glanced again at the report in front of him and added, "No name was given with the tip. Only the room number."

"The murderer had to have been someone who didn't know Edward Garrett well," Trixie said slowly as she scanned her notes.

The officer looked at her curiously. Trixie continued, "He would never have ordered a steak dinner. He was in his vegetarian phase, and if you knew Edward, you would know nothing or no one could make him order a steak dinner. And why only one? It certainly couldn't have been a late night supper to share with Stephanie Sweet. Who ordered it?"

The officer frowned and grabbed his desk phone. He called room service and requested they check on a steak dinner ordered the evening of Edward's murder and delivered to his room. Trixie smiled and chatted a few more minutes about the particulars of the case when the phone rang.

It was room service. The meal had been ordered earlier in the afternoon from room 232 – Tyra Field's room. The request had specified 1:30 AM as the delivery time.

Trixie checked her dance schedule and determined the time of the order was the same time Tyra and Tino were on the dance floor competing. "I suppose whoever is setting Tyra up for this murder didn't expect you to check on the time of the order, but it was ordered using Tyra's stolen keycard and at a time when the murderer wouldn't have been interrupted. That leaves both Tyra and Tino off the hook."

The officer smiled. This woman was certainly going to help his department with this case. Yes, indeed.

"See if you can trace the call about the knife. I would be surprised if it was made by the cleaning crew. Who cleans a room in the middle of the night?" She stood and fluttered her fingers at the officer. "Keep in touch."

"Do me a favor?" the officer stood and handed her his card. "Put my number on speed dial." She chuckled and left to find Tino Van Arp.

There were several adjoining ballrooms set up for the competition. With so many routines on the schedule, there were simultaneous dance heats going on in both rooms. The changing areas were outside the ballrooms along with a large open space housing the vendor booths.

Trixie walk past the booths to the first ballroom. She glanced quickly around the large room to the tables along the dance floor hoping to spot the Minneapolis dance delegation. They were not in the first ballroom, so she moved on to the second smaller space. She spotted a table of students and waved as she caught the eye of one elderly student. Moving around the room, she scanned the table for Tino. As she approached the table, the students rose and engulfed her in hugs.

"What are you doing here?" There was a buzz of conversation going as she clasps hands with several of them.

"I'm trying to settle this horrible murder situation," Trixie explained shaking her head and sounding very mournful. No use not telling them the real reason for her trip to Las Vegas. It was a partial truth. "Have any of you seen Tino Van Arp?"

One pointed out to the dance floor at the group dancing a Tango. Indeed he was out on the floor with one of his students. They seemed to be one of the top couples on the floor. Their patterns were dramatic and sharp as they passed the table of Minneapolis supporters who cheered wildly at their corte move. Trixie smiled and joined in the claps. Tino's slim build looked perfect on the large floor as he skillfully maneuvered his student into a series of quick fans. His student was wearing a lovely dance dress with long sleeves and a glittery fitted bodice that flared to a skirt with layers of soft floating fabric. It was ideal for a Tango and caught the attention of the judges who were circling the perimeter of the dance floor. She spotted Carl Friend across the room pursing his lips and staring at another couple in front of him. He began to furiously write on his pad then glanced toward the next couple circling the floor toward his corner.

Tino and his student did very well taking second place in a field of eleven couples. Each heat was divided into couples of the same dance level, age and sex. At the end of each heat, the places were announced and awards dispersed. Tino's head bobbed cheerfully as they were announced as the second place winners. It brought him that much closer to an award for the top male teachers. He might make it into the top ten if he was lucky. There were quite a number of male teachers with more experience than Tino Van Arp. He escorted his student off the floor and back to the Minneapolis table clapping at their approach. It was then he spotted Trixie.

She pulled him to the side for a private conversation. "What are you doing here?" he blurted out when they were far enough away from the rest of the group.

"I'm here to solve this murder and your butt," she announced crisply. "I need your key card. I'm going to stay in your room – your first unoccupied room."

He flipped open his dance bag and pawed through the side pockets for the card. Trixie noticed the cards didn't have room numbers. This card was a plain card with the hotel logo on the front.

"How do you know that is the right key?" she asked in a whisper.

"I put each of my room cards in different pockets. See. Here is the card for Tyra's room," he produced a similar looking card from a second pocket. "By the way. I think Tyra has been arrested for Edward's murder. There was a news story on the TV about the arrest. Have you seen her yet? Is she OK? I don't know how they can plant this on her. She has an airtight alibi."

Trixie debated how much to tell Tino. Could she trust him? She didn't know. Best not to give him too much information. "So do you know anything that could help her case?" she asked instead.

"Other than we were both in custody when the murder was supposed to have taken place?" He shook his head. "I don't know what else I can say."

"How about Carl Friend?" Trixie nodded her head toward the staunch round man in the corner.

"The judge? That Carl Friend? Well he doesn't seem to be a friend to me. He gave my last student low enough scores that placed us second rather than first which is what we deserved!" Tino seemed somewhat put off and glared at the man with the bald head and gray fringe of hair circling his protruding ears. It was indeed hard to imagine Carl Friend as a former dance champion – which he was. Today Carl was neither slim nor in shape to even perform a competent Tango routine. His belly fell over his belted waist and his jowl bulged above his dress shirt collar and black tie. Trixie tried to remember how long she had known Carl Friend and just why she so vividly remembered the man.

On to the next number on the list – settle into her room and find this Stephanie Sweet person. Trixie paid careful attention to the path she took to Tino's room. It was room number 239. The one side of the hall had even numbers and the other odd. It was only two floors up from the main level with the ballrooms, so no need for an elevator – just a quick walk up the stairs. Tyra's room was across the hall and a couple of rooms down. Trixie made note of this as she inserted the card and opened the door. Edward's room was up a floor. He had a corner suite.

Tino's room seemed to be untouched, but Trixie carefully searched all of the wastebaskets and corners before tossing her purse on the bed. She pulled out her toothbrush still packaged along with the new toothpaste and deodorant she had purchased before boarding the plane to get her through a few days. She splashed water on her face and stared at the bags under her eyes. No matter what she did, the wrinkles never seemed to go away. That was the problem with aging. She patted her stick straight hair into place and fluffed the back a bit. No time to take a nap just yet although her body was drawn toward the comfortable bed. Later – after a chat with Stephanie Sweet and Carl Friend. She would have to seek out Mrs. Crawford as well although she wondered why Tyra was insistent about putting the elderly woman on the suspect list. Putting the key card back into her bag, Trixie headed out the door and to the first floor restaurant.

The hotel was a mass of Las Vegas glitz. The lobby area was surrounded on the one side by the ballroom and entertainment areas. The casino was on the other side with both areas divided by a spacious and elegant restaurant. The entrance to the restaurant was casual with barstools hugging a counter and a number of round tall tables. Then the carpeting led toward a more stylish area for the serious diner. The low tables had white crisp tablecloths, centerpieces of fresh flowers and crystal chandeliers. They definitely tried to cover all guests adequately with the casual front and the pricy back. Trixie chose a stool at the bar and waited for the bartender to slap down a napkin for her order. She asked for a Diet Coke and a lunch menu. The special seemed safe enough – a tuna melt with a cup of wild rice soup. Sounded like home!

When the bartender brought her order, she asked him about Stephanie. He nodded toward a tall woman in a low cut form fitting uniform. Very Las Vegas Trixie thought. Yes, Stephanie Sweet was definitely Edward Garrett's type. There was nothing surprising here. Stephanie was waiting on a tired looking man who must have been up all night in the casino. She was pouring him cup after cup of black coffee and chatting cheerfully with a brilliant white toothed smile. Her sunny red colored hair was long with a bang dipping over a heavily made up eye. Anyone who knew Edward at all would know Stephanie Sweet was someone he would find attractive — although Trixie thought her to be a bit busty for Edward. He tended to gravitate toward the more slender model–types.

Trixie finished her meal, paid her bill and meandered over toward Stephanie who was now at the beverage station filling a water glass.

"Hi, I'm Trixie Appleby. I'm Edward Garrett's secretary. Do you have a few minutes to talk with me?" Trixie had carefully noted there were no more customers in the restaurant at this time.

At first Stephanie seemed shocked and disturbed by Trixie's presence, but Trixie chirped on about how long she had worked for Edward and how saddened she was by his death. Soon Stephanie was sitting down at a table with Trixie and pouring out her sad story of finding the body and how upsetting it was. Stephanie was indeed young, and it appeared this was Stephanie's first encounter with death. She had gotten off work around quarter to two and took time to change her clothes before going up to Edward's room. She knew immediately something was wrong because of all the blood all over the bed where Edward was sprawled. She dialed 911 and security had arrived in a few minutes. She waited outside in the hall for them to get to the room.

"I didn't touch anything. Nothing at all," she shook her head violently back and forth as if to convince Trixie. Trixie nodded in all the right places of Stephanie's story and patted her hand comforting her at exactly the right time. Stephanie was soon pouring out more and more details, but Trixie had the feeling there was something Stephanie was not saying. Something was remaining a secret.

"And how did you meet Mr. Garrett? Was he a customer in the restaurant?" Trixie asked in a soft soothing voice gazing into Stephanie's tearful eyes.

"No. I met him at the dance competition. We just clicked," she began to smile and stare off past Trixie.

"Do you remember anything about the room service cart? Was he ordering dinner for you?" Trixie prodded a little further.

Stephanie frowned. "No, I wasn't hungry. We usually are able to eat a meal during our shift. But I do remember there was a cart in front of the bed. I think the plate was covered with a metal warming cover. I don't remember a glass or beverage, but it could have been on the tray I guess. No. I'm afraid I don't recall very much about the room other than seeing the blood and the body. It was quite horrifying." She began to shudder with a quick twitch of her facial expression.

"Had you gone up to the room before your work shift?" Trixie slowly eased into the conversation.

"No. We watched the dancing, and I told Edward I had to work, so he gave me the keycard and told me to come up to the room after my shift ended. We'd hang out, and he'd teach me to dance," she softened a bit as she recalled their plans.

Yes, that sounded like a typical Edward Garrett line to a beautiful young girl. Trixie's eye narrowed, and she found herself twisting her mouth into a sarcastic frown. "Well, thank you very much. I appreciate your story. We are all trying to get through this tragedy as best we can. If you think of anything – anything at all, just let me know. I'll be around for a few days taking care of the arrangements for the funeral." She let her eyes lower into a somber sadness. Stephanie Sweet returned the sad face with a mournful look and watched Trixie leave.

Trixie wandered back to the competition. She was looking for Carl Friend or Mrs. Crawford when she spotted the vendor booths and remembered she needed to buy a few dresses for the event so she wouldn't look too haphazard and out of place. She stopped at a few booths looking at the jewelry and dance shoes. She fingered a dance bag and spotted a cover up shawl that looked a bit pricy. Moving on, she glanced around looking for Karen Danbury's booth. Karen was back in a corner chatting with a potential customer who was choosing fabric swatches from a sample book.

Trixie and Karen had worked together for a number of years, but in different studios. So a close friendship had not developed. They were instead business associates. Trixie pushed past a heavily stoned glitzy gown with feathers along the bottom of the skirt to some of the dresses with a less performance appearance. There were a few for sale on consignment with fairly inexpensive price tags. She pulled out a lavender dress with long sleeves and a floating skirt. It was trimmed with gold braid along the neckline and wrists. She also snatched a second dress. It was a sleeveless black sheath with a beaded jacket. There was a changing area in the back corner with curtains dividing each area. Trixie tried on both dresses and standing in front of the narrow mirror in the changing area found each to fit nicely. Would she have chosen something else if she were not desperate? Oh yes. But purchasing these dresses also gave her a chance to glean some info from Karen. She was the perfect person to hear some of the gossip concerning Edward Garrett's murder. People always chatted when trying on dresses.

Karen Danbury was finally free. Her client had ordered her dress and was on to the next booth to find a piece of jewelry to match the ordered gown. Trixie walked up with dresses in hand and the two women embraced affectionately.

"Long time no see," Karen greeted. "And what a time we're having." She shook her head. "I never thought this dance competition would bring such drama."

"That's why I'm here," Trixie confessed. "It's been quite a shock for the whole studio. How are you doing? How's business?"

Karen smiled. She had aged since Trixie last saw her. She was always a slight woman, but the wrinkles on Karen's face just like on Trixie's were spreading. "I'm doing very well. I love this business. I'm now able to travel to more competitions for orders and to sell off stock. I meet lots of wonderful dancers. I feel … well, creative. I'm always busy." Karen fingered the dresses Trixie had chosen lovingly.

"How's the hubby? Does he like this dress business more than the dancing?" Trixie didn't know if Karen's husband had liked or disliked her teaching at the studio. Karen never seemed to mention anything.

"Oh, he loves this! We're able to do so much traveling. He is one who loves to get out and about." She let her thin lips spread into a wide grin.

"I'll take these two dresses," Trixie nodded and continued. "I had to leave Minneapolis so quickly I didn't have time to pack." They both laughed, and Karen gave her a generous discount.

"Did you happen to see Edward with anyone when he was here at the competition? There was a young woman who found his body. Did you happen to see her?" Trixie fished for gossip.

"No. I can't say that I did. I didn't really see much of Edward when he was around. Dresses aren't his thing I guess," Karen laughed as she put Trixie's purchases into a bag.

XIV.

Trixie took her dresses back to her room and in spite of her desire to solve this murder thing as quickly as possible decided a nap was necessary. She was so tired she could hardly keep her eyes open. With the flight and the stress of the murder, her body was slowly shutting down. Why hadn't she brought pajamas or a t-shirt for sleeping? She would have to pick up a Las Vegas shirt from the gift store. Climbing out of her clothes, she snuggled into bed and pulled the covers up to her neck. As she faded away thoughts from her list began to circle in her head, but they quickly disappeared as all went dark. She woke around dinner time and felt refreshed. Hopping into the shower, she made a note of the little items she would have to purchase from the hotel gift shop. These two dresses were certainly a help, but there were all the other things – underwear, pajamas, etc. that were becoming more important. She felt wonderful after the shower and quickly styled her hair and fixed her makeup.

Pulling out her notebook, she ripped out the page and began a new list. 1. Check with police on the knife call. 2. Carl Friend. 3. Mrs. Crawford. 4. Talk again with Stephanie Sweet. 5. Review progress with Tyra. She reread the list and nodded. Adequate!

Trixie slipped into the black dress and snatched her purse for a quick trip to the hotel gift shop. As she exited the room, she noticed the woman sauntering down the hall pushing the room service cart. "Excuse me!" She called after the woman who seemed to ignore her calls. Trotting down the hall, she managed to get the woman's attention. "Excuse me, do you always deliver room service in the evening?"

The woman was short with dark hair wearing a white uniform – not the same style as worn by Stephanie Sweet however. The woman looked up into Trixie's face and appeared not to understand what she was saying. The walkie talkie on her belt began to squawk loudly, and Trixie noticed the language spoken over the square was Spanish. "Habla Espanol?" Trixie didn't know much Spanish, but this question did get a big response from the woman. She smiled broadly and began to spout a fast conversation that Trixie could not understand. She held up her hand and tried to communicate with hand gestures. Finally, she just followed the woman to the delivery and waited for her to deposit the cart to the customer and accept a small tip. Then Trixie followed her down to the kitchen where she might find someone who spoke both Spanish and English.

"Do you speak English?" Trixie gestured wildly to a man who seemed to be the woman's boss. He nodded and smiled. "Could you translate for me?" Trixie asked as the woman and her boss stood facing each other with occasional glances at the animated Trixie.

"Could you ask her if she delivers room service to the third floor in the evenings?" Trixie directed toward the man. He seemed to successfully relay her message to the woman who nodded her head "yes". "Did you deliver a steak meal the other evening to room 334 around one or 1:30 AM?" The man again relayed the question, and the woman again nodded.

Trixie smiled broadly. "Who accepted the delivery? Was it a man?" The question was passed along, and this time the woman began to spout a long explanation in Spanish using her hands to go into further detail.

Finally the man turned to Trixie and explained in broken English. "She said there was a man who came to the door, but a woman had already come down the hall to give her a large tip for the delivery and ask her to 'forget everything about this delivery'."

"Then what happened?" Trixie's eyes grew larger.

"The woman took the cart and knocked on the door. Luz Maria noticed as she looked back that the man came to the door and looked surprised to see the cart and the woman. She was afraid to say anything because the next day someone told her the man in room 334 had been murdered. She didn't know what to do." The boss was definitely a bit upset by this admission, but continued to translate between the two women.

"What did the woman look like?" Trixie was quite excited she might get a surprising break in this case. The woman frowned at this next question. She didn't seem to be able to describe the woman. "How tall was she?" Trixie asked. "Tall" came back the reply. But as Trixie thought about another question to ask she looked down at the top of the tiny woman's head and decided anyone would seem tall to this little lady. That didn't give Trixie much of a description.

"If I bring a few photos, would you be able to pick out a face?" Trixie held her breath. Without even relaying the question, the man turned to Trixie and promised her the woman would look at the photos. Trixie thanked the two and hurried back to the main floor to meet with the police once again.

Trixie explained what had just happened to the officer in charge, and he listened patiently to her plan. Get a few photos and ask Luz Maria to identify the person. Just who did she have in mind? Trixie felt she was taking a step backwards – who should be in the photo line-up? Ok, so Tyra should definitely be in the photo grouping. Mrs. Crawford? She sighed. Hardly! Stephanie Sweet? Maybe. Suddenly the task seemed overwhelming. The detective said he would try to put together a photo grouping and was quite interested in talking with the woman about what she saw. Trixie left his office with mixed feelings. Had she opened up a new clue or a dead end?

On to the next task. Trixie wandered into the hotel gift shop and went to the section reserved for forgotten items. She picked up a package of generic white underpants and a t-shirt with enough length to use as a nightgown. There a few makeup items she needed and a pair of pantyhose. After she purchased her necessities, she went to the lobby to call Tyra. Tyra must be bored by now. Stuck in her room with just the TV! But before she could dial the number, a call came in on her phone. It was the detective. He informed her Luz Maria had disappeared. The news gave Trixie a nervous start. Had the murderer discovered the woman as well and gotten rid of the witness? No, the detective explained Luz Maria had most likely been an illegal alien. Her boss said she had become nervous with the questions and decided to quit her job before the authorities brought her in for more questions. Trixie sighed. A dead end indeed!

A few minutes later, Trixie was once again sitting in the comfy chair chatting with Tyra. Tyra was curled up on the bed in her pajamas with no makeup. Her spirits were down. She looked pale and seemed to appreciate Trixie's visit. Trixie told her about her conversation with Luz

Maria. Tyra became initially excited until Trixie told her about her disappearance. Then she reviewed her conversation with Stephanie Sweet. "I think she's hiding something," Trixie admitted.

"What?" Tyra leaned back impatiently and closed her eyes. The whole situation seemed to bore her.

"I don't know, but I'm going to find her again and have another conversation. Do you have suggestions for a few new questions?" Trixie had her notebook out. Tyra shrugged her shoulders.

"I wonder if Stephanie Sweet is her real name. Maybe she has a record. She said she had never met Edward before. I guess that is possible, but I find it hard to believe she went to the dance competition on her own just to watch the dancers. It's not something someone would just stop by to watch. I feel there was a reason she was there. I wonder what that reason could be." Trixie let the thoughts float around in her head before she left. Tyra seemed to need a little extra attention today so Trixie sat for a while longer. Tyra's normal upright posture was hunched, and her eyes scanned the room not focusing on anything in particular. This concerned Trixie. This concerned her very much.

There was a cocktail party and dinner that evening before the professional competition. The ballroom was elegant. Tables sported linen table cloths and fresh flower centerpieces. Crowds of dancers dressed in sleek evening dresses and tuxedos held fluted champagne glasses. Trixie felt comfortable mingling with the Minneapolis group. She needed to scope out Mrs. Crawford as well as Carl Friend. Carl was across the room talking with a few of the other judges. He must not be judging that evening. He was dressed rather casually in a sport coat and dress shirt with no tie. Trixie moved away from the Minneapolis group and toward Carl. She waved as she approached, and his face lit up.

"Well, Miss Appleby," he greeted. "How is Minneapolis these days?"

Trixie and Carl had met years ago when they both were a bit younger. In those days, Carl was dark haired and handsome. Trixie was considered stylish and "cute". They both could dance circles around anyone else on the floor. Now they watched the younger dancers doing the circles and sighed remembering days long past.

Carl smiled and greeted Trixie with a hug and peck on the cheek. "Judging this event I see," Trixie said with a wave of her hand around the room.

"That's what I do," he replied flippantly. "These days that is." There was sadness in his tone. "The hay days of being the star are long gone." His lips flattened into plastic grin.

"And Edward Garrett?" Trixie thought she would get to the point quickly.

Carl frowned and stared into her face. "I'm sorry Edward is dead." His voice was unenthusiastic and his face pinched.

"I don't think you are sorry at all," Trixie shot back in a sharp tone. She had hit a nerve.

"Edward and I didn't get along. You know that. Everyone knows that. It's been years of dislike. It's been mutual. He never liked me either." His eyes narrowed darkly, and he shrugged his shoulders signaling for another drink from the waitress. She brought a tray of champagne glasses, and he took one for himself in one hand and a second for Trixie in the other. Trixie accepted the glass and took a sip watching closely for Carl's expression to change.

"Edward Garrett is dead. Maybe now you can tell me what happened between the two of you." Trixie asked if Carl wanted to sit down at one of the tables away from the crowd. Carl hesitated and shook his head. He turned and walked back to the other judges. Trixie smiled. She knew he would confide in her after he thought about it. It would just take him a little time to make that decision. It would nag on his soul until he opened up to someone, and she would be waiting.

She turned back toward the Minneapolis group. On to Mrs. Crawford. Mrs. Crawford was having a lively conversation with a few of the other competitors. She looked stunning for an older woman dressed in a stoned long sleeve top of teal blue over a floating skirt of white silk. Her

138

satin heels were dyed the exact same shade as her top. She wore an expensive diamond necklace and matching earrings. Trixie waited for a lull in the conversation to ask if they could talk. Mrs. Crawford looked curiously surprised but followed Trixie to a quiet back corner of the room.

"As you know I'm here because my dear boss, Edward Garrett was murdered," Trixie began the conversation. Mrs. Crawford nodded with a lift of one neatly plucked eyebrow. "Have you heard any gossip or talk about the murder?"

Mrs. Crawford seemed pleased that Trixie would come to her for information. She gushed on a bit about how shocked people were but claimed to have no concrete news from anyone about any further details other than the TV report that a suspect had been arrested. In a quiet whisper she confided, "I think they've arrested Tyra Vessi for the murder." She used Tyra's married name when speaking of her. She was clearly one who believed in a woman taking her husband's name.

"I understand you weren't very fond of Tyra," Trixie inquired with hesitation not wanting Mrs. Crawford to close up.

"Well, it wasn't that I wasn't fond of Mrs. Vessi but rather that I was fond of Mr. Vessi. After all, he was my teacher." She smiled lifting her chest proudly at the statement.

"As it should be," Trixie agreed. "You had a conversation with Mr. Van Arp about Mr. Vessi yesterday?"

At first she frowned then as if something suddenly clicked in her brain she smiled broadly. "Oh, yes. After seeing that Miss Jensen the other day, it just reminded me so much of Mr. Vessi. They were a much better couple than Tyra and Cameron. They didn't fight and seemed to be so happy. Mrs. Vessi wasn't suited for Mr. Vessi — too old and always arguing. That Miss Jensen would have been a much better partner for Mr. Vessi in both dancing and in life!" Mrs. Crawford stated her opinion quite clearly and with great confidence.

"You say you saw Miss Jensen? Here in Las Vegas?" Trixie repeated. She thought she must have heard incorrectly. Mrs. Crawford was an older woman, and her sight must be playing tricks on her mind.

"Why yes! I saw her walking into the restaurant one morning when I was heading back to my room to pick up another pair of shoes," Mrs. Crawford nodded her head quite confident in her recollection.

"Was that before Edward — Mr. Garrett was murdered?" Trixie wanted badly to pull out her notebook and jot a few notes but instead kept a steady eye on Mrs. Crawford and her reactions.

"Oh my yes! I know it was her. It surprised me because I knew she hadn't traveled with our group. I wanted to go up to her and say

140

something, but she seemed to disappear just when I got to the restaurant. Into thin air!" Her hand went up, and she snapped her fingers. Her head began to shake slightly from side to side.

Was Mrs. Crawford mistaken? Had she seen someone who reminded her of Jordan Jensen? Is that why she began the conversation with Tino regarding Cameron and Jordan? Was it coincidence? Trixie's mind began to whirl into new directions. She thanked Mrs. Crawford for the conversation and hurried back to the hallway to make a quick call. Checking the clock, she tried to calculate what time it would be back in Minneapolis. She dialed the studio number and was greeted by Ashley Arthur's pleasant voice, "Studio!"

"How is everything going back in Minnesota?" she began. The news was typical. Ashley related a few tidbits about lessons taught before Trixie changed the subject and asked about Jordan Jensen. "Has Jordan been in the studio while I've been gone?" Yes, of course Ashley related in a crisp tone. And as Trixie recalled, she was in the studio during the time of Edward's murder. In fact she had worked with her on one of her lesson plans that very day. "Could you put Jordan on the phone, please?" she requested. Jordan was on a lesson she was told, but Ashley would have her call as soon as she was done. Trixie hung up the phone and pondered. What did this last development mean? Calculating in her head she began to think everything through very carefully. Jordan worked part-time in the studio from six in the evening until ten. Yes, Jordan worked the evening

141

Edward was murdered. But he was killed around one thirty in the morning. Could Jordan have flown to Las Vegas after ten in the evening, arrived to kill Edward by one thirty and fly back to Minneapolis before six the next evening? Of course! But how could Mrs. Crawford have seen Jordan in the morning before Edward's death? Trixie pondered. Her eyes circled the lobby of the hotel. She gazed toward the restaurant where Mrs. Crawford claimed to have seen Jordan Jensen — also where Stephanie Sweet worked. Her eyes continued toward the hotel front desk.

Moving quickly toward the desk, she leaned forward and with a charming smile asked, "Is there a travel agency nearby?"

The answer was a pleasant nod and directions toward a small shop outside the front door. Trixie asked for flight information to and from Las Vegas and Minneapolis for the past two days. Glancing at the times of departure and arrival, she calculated which flights were possible for Jordan Jensen to travel between the two cities within the necessary time frame. Carefully tucking this information into her purse, she headed toward the security office and a quick meeting with an officer. She presented her information regarding the sighting of Jordan Jensen. The officer looked on curiously as Trixie explained who Jordan Jensen was and why she would be a suspect in this murder. Jordan was definitely someone who had something to gain by Tyra Fields Vessi's arrest and conviction as a murderer. There were problems with this, however. Trixie explained the time element of this theory. She asked if the police could check flight lists for Jordan Jensen on the days before and after the murder making her appearance in Las Vegas a possibility.

The whole Jordan Jensen theory was something Trixie decided was not one she wanted to share just yet with Tyra. She knew the emotion just the name brought to Tyra. Sitting in the lobby, Trixie became more agitated by the minute. She had not yet received a call from Jordan. Trixie tapped her finger tips on the top of the table next to the overstuffed chair. She carefully checked her watch and calculated the time differences. Finally, she picked up her phone and called the studio. Once again Ashley's pleasant voice picked up.

"Mr. Arthur, I haven't received a call yet from Jordan Jensen." Trixie found her voice tone to be irritated and short.

"Oh, my," Ashley gasped in his high pitched wheeze. "I totally forgot to give her the message. She's gone I'm afraid. I'm the only one left. It was such a busy hectic night." He began to make excuses with a droning tone to his voice. Trixie found herself not even listening anymore. His voice became a buzz of non-words.

Trixie sighed. "Give me her home number, please." She knew contacting Jordan Jensen was imperative to her case. Jordan was the pivot point in turning this whole situation in a different direction. Copying down Jordan's number, she carefully dialed. No one home yet. She would have to try back again later. Maybe she had enough time to try again with Carl Friend.

Looking around the ballroom, she spotted Carl in a lively conversation with another judge. Both looked hostile and angry. Obviously Edward Garrett was not the only person with whom Carl had difficulty. Keeping an eye on the pair, Trixie moved toward the Minneapolis group again. They were crowded around a table laughing and holding their cocktail glasses. One of the students had placed a large photo album on the table. Her husband was an avid photographer and had managed to already develop several rolls of photos from the Las Vegas competition. He had mounted the photos in a lovely bound book with "Las Vegas" gold etched in the cover. There were other albums around the table, and the books were certainly creating topics of conversation among the competitors. Dancers from other studios were now crowding around the table as well. Trixie spotted one book labeled "Studio Events" and snatching it up. Finding a seat at another table, she began to flip through the pages. What was she hoping to find? There were photos of Tyra with all her different hair colors. Trixie found herself chuckling. There were some pictures of Tyra and Cameron. Tears began to well in Trixie's eyes as she carefully gazed on the older images. Flipping the page, she came upon a staff photo, and yes, there was Jordan Jensen smiling in the middle row. Her hair was different — probably why Tyra never recognized the woman upon her return to the studio after Cameron's death. But the face was clearly recognizable. She flipped to the next page and found another photo of the staff routine danced when Jordan was a downtown staff member. There she was in one of the photos striking a lovely pose. Trixie motioned for the photographer to join her table for a moment. "Could I have these two photos for a few moments?"

The man looked curiously at Trixie's pleading eyes and nodded with a frown. Trixie grabbed his sleeve as he was about to return to the group. She added, "Could we keep this our little secret, please?" This startled him all the more. He cocked his head to the side as if in thought. "It's about the murder," Trixie explained further. "Top secret!" Then she flashed a pleading smile. She hoped he would value this explanation but realized it would now be the subject of gossip. Glancing at the photos again, she wondered if he would realize which person in the photo she found interesting. Hopefully not!

Carefully taking the two photos, she slid them into her purse and slipped off to the security office once again. She sighed. This was becoming a common path, but she had promised to share any and all information she gleaned. She also recognized if she became too close to the truth, she herself might be at risk. Before entering the office, she quickly redialed Jordan Jensen's number. This time Jordan answered the phone.

What was she going to ask Jordan without tipping her off the real motive for the questions? She began with a few questions about her lessons that evening and the student Trixie had helped with the other night. Jordan answered all questions but had a slight sound of confusion to her voice. Why would Trixie Appleby call her at home so late in the evening? This was certainly odd, and Trixie would have to address this concern.

"Honestly Jordan, I called the studio earlier asking Ashley to have you call me ASAP. I found out he never gave you the message. I need to ask you a few questions as we attempt to finalize Edward's murder." Trixie thought that sounded quite official. Jordan agreed enthusiastically to this explanation. "They have arrested a suspect in the murder," Trixie continued. This should alleviate any worries about the next few questions Trixie decided. "By the way, have you ever been to Las Vegas?" She asked this as a way of introduction to the questions to follow. Jordan claimed she hadn't. "Well, then some of the questions I will be asking may be a bit difficult to answer ..." Trixie sighed as if she was thinking through some of her next questions. "Well, this may seem strange then. But do you know Carl Friend? He's a dance judge." Jordan said she had never heard of Carl Friend. "Ok. Then have you heard the name Stephanie Sweet?" Again Jordan claimed not to know anyone by that name. "Have you ever heard Mrs. Crawford mention any of these people?" Jordan was silent for a few seconds. She clearly knew Mrs.

Crawford. "To explain a bit more about this last question, Mrs. Crawford seems to be quite fond of you and has talked quite openly about you during this trip. I thought maybe in conversations with her she may have mentioned some of these people of interest. Do you recall any mention of these people in conversations with Mrs. Crawford?" Jordan hesitated but then answered with a negative response.

Jordan seemed to open up a bit after this question. "I'm glad Mrs. Crawford is fond of me, but truthfully I don't really remember much of anything she has said about anything or anyone. I try to humor her when she starts to babble on about people. Idle gossip. That's all it is, and I don't want to be a part of it."

Trixie thought this reply very noble, but it was certainly the response Jordan expected Trixie wanted to hear. Jordan had no idea Trixie's real question was about Jordan's sighting in Las Vegas and her real interest was in Jordan's response to her question about ever being in the city. Trixie smiled and thanked Jordan. "I'll contact you if I have any other questions. Maybe you could find out from others on the staff if they have heard Mrs. Crawford mention these names as well? I trust you can do that and call me tomorrow if you find out anything of importance." Jordan seemed very pleased to be put in charge of this "very important" task.

Trixie brought the photos to the police, and they made copies. They reported no one by the name of "Jordan Jensen" was on any flight list to or from Las Vegas to Minneapolis during the past two days. Trixie sighed. What did this mean? Trixie asked for copies of the photos as well. She wanted to ask Stephanie Sweet if she knew Jordan. It was a long shot but there must be a tie in someplace. Trixie went down her list, but this time she marked the problems with each of her suspects.

Mrs. Crawford. The more Trixie thought about Mrs. Crawford, the more it appeared she was simply a fluffy old lady who was more interested in gossip than murder. Trixie also thought Mrs. Crawford would be one Luz Maria would have recognized right away if she was the woman she met when delivering the dinner tray to Edward's room. How could you not realize a woman was a blue haired older woman? No disguise could hide that.

Carl Friend. He was definitely someone who hated both Edward and Tyra. His opinion of Tyra was most likely due to his feud with Edward. Whatever the cause of this bad blood was something Trixie would certainly have to delve into more deeply. But Carl was not a woman. He would have had to have an accomplice to murder Edward Garrett.

Stephanie Sweet. Here was a woman who appeared not to have met Edward Garrett before the day of his murder. She was someone who had an alibi for the exact time of the murder. She was working. Would she have something against Tyra – or even know who Tyra Fields was? How would she get Tyra's room key?

Jordan Jensen. Jordan had the time and opportunity to get back and forth between Minneapolis and Las Vegas to murder Edward. She also had something against Tyra – certainly enough animosity to put the blame on Tyra. But she couldn't have made the call for the steak dinner during the afternoon when Tyra and Tino were competing on the dance floor. She would also have known with certainty that Edward Garrett was a practicing vegetarian. She was on the staff after all and no one – no one – could miss his recent ranting about the evils of meat. She also claimed she had never been to Las Vegas. The flight records pulled by the police seemed to verify this statement.

Tyra and Tino? Neither was able to either murder Edward or make the call for the room service. They both had air tight alibis. Extremely air tight!

Trixie sighed. What next? It was time for dinner. Competition dinners always began later than most, and she really needed to speak again with Carl Friend. Maybe this would be an ideal time for a more private conversation. She returned to the ballroom now set up with elegantly decorated china place settings for dinner. Scanning the groups as they circled the tables finding seats, Trixie debated whether it was more

149

productive to sit with the Minneapolis group and possibly hear a few tidbits of gossip or find Carl and ask him to be her dinner "date". She decided she'd find Carl. She spotted him in the corner. He noticed her approaching. Was his expression one of joy or agitation? It was hard to tell from this distance. She tried to put on her most pleasant expression. "Care for a dinner partner?" she purred.

Twisting his mouth, Carl Friend debated. "Are you trying to get more information out of me?"

"Of course!" Trixie retorted with a glowing smile.

Carl reared in surprise and with a hearty laugh responded. "Sure. Why not?"

They joined a table of studio executives and judges. Trixie was quite used to this. She'd attended more than her share of owner/executive meetings with many of these same people over the years. The first few minutes Carl seemed on edge and hardly said a word to Trixie directly. Trixie joined in the conversations about the new syllabus scheduled to come out next year and the national competition where some of the patterns would be premiered in the scheduled dance sessions for the professionals. Trixie was glad she had purchased the little black dress from Karen's consignment inventory. It was perfect for this event. She leaned back comfortably and smoothed her napkin in her lap.

Eventually the conversation got around to Edward Garrett's murder. One by one the group injected their "sincere sympathy" for Trixie and her staff for their loss. Some asked for any new details on solving the case. Trixie decided to remain silent and give no tidbits of information, but many had their own interpretation of the event. Mob hit was one suggestion, and domestic problem was another from someone who evidently didn't know that Edward was not married. The last comment brought a few snickers from some who knew better. The subject slowly died to an uncomfortable silence until the conversation moved on to the problems with the Atlanta studio. At this point Trixie turned toward Carl.

"So that was uncomfortable," Trixie sighed. "Although it is a difficult situation, most haven't made comments on Edward's redeeming qualities." Both she and Carl laughed. "No Edward seemed to make more than his share of enemies. One of whom seems to be you," Trixie chose her words carefully. Her words were spoken with a slow but quiet tone.

Carl Friend smiled faintly. "Edward and I had a mutual dislike for each other. He was jealous of me, and I of him." He shrugged and continued before Trixie could ask any questions. "I was a champion dancer. Edward always wanted to be but never was. He couldn't keep a partner – in dance or in life. He was a lonely man. I had everything he wanted. A dance partner, a championship title, and a wife. I had everything he wanted." Carl suddenly sat back smugly and closed his eyes remembering.

"So what did he have that you wanted?" Trixie asked gently.

"My wife," his voice was quiet and sad. "He took my wife. That ended my marriage, my dance partnership and my dance titles. He took everything. And why? Just to see if he could. He didn't have any intention of keeping up a relationship with Irma. He just wanted a short term fling. And that's what he got. A roll in the hay broke up a marriage and a long time dance career. Sad. Very sad."

"Yes indeed," Trixie mourned along with Carl Friend. She recalled that Irma and Carl Friend were at one time the top dance couple in the United States. They were unbeatable. Suddenly they were gone. No one knew what happened – no one but evidently Edward Garrett who said nothing of the matter to Trixie Appleby. She knew Edward had his secrets, but this one seemed to be right up there with one of the most despicable. Did Carl Friend have reason to kill Edward Garrett? Most certainly. Did she believe he did it? No, not really. He was more the type to make comments behind Edward's back and brood in silence than do something violent. She put her hand on his forearm and simply said, "I'm sorry, Carl. Very sorry." They stared into each others' eyes for a moment and then went on to discuss more pleasant subjects. The meal was actually quite enjoyable and for a short time, Trixie forgot the real reason she was here in Las Vegas.

The dinner finished with a lovely dessert of chocolate mousse with strawberries and coffee all around. There would be a dance for a few hours and some professional routines by some of the big names in the dance world. Trixie couldn't help but think about the days when Carl and Irma Friend would have been the couple out on the floor performing for the group. Now he sat back in his chair letting his belly fold over his belt and felt sorry for what could have been. They were both growing older, and this show would remind them of their age more than anything else ever could.

Trixie excuses herself and headed toward the rest room. She paused thinking about her next move. She had eliminated Carl Friend as suspect – at least in her own mind. What would she do now? She decided to pass around the photo of Jordan Jensen to see if anyone recalled seeing her. The Minneapolis group would be suspicious if she asked them about Jordan, but someone who might not know the woman would be a better choice. She headed immediately to the restaurant and found Stephanie Sweet refilling waters for a table of new customers. Patiently waiting until she had completed her task, Trixie moved in.

"I know you are working and don't want to bother you…"

"Then don't!" Stephanie was agitated by the intrusion. She was clearly busy with a few tables of hungry gamblers.

"Just a moment of your time," Trixie continued quickly. "Have you ever seen this woman?" She shoved one of the photos in front of Stephanie's nose.

Stephanie reeled back to get a better look at the picture. Squinting she seemed less agitated and now more nervous. "Nope. Never seen her before," she turned to grab the coffee pot.

"Sure of that?" Trixie prodded.

"Yup. Sure," Stephanie turned abruptly and scurried off with the pot of coffee in hand.

Trixie watched her for a moment and then decided Stephanie was simply tired of the whole Edward Garrett situation. She shrugged and wandered back to the ballroom. The vendors were hawking their wares to the dancers who were in the mood to spend money. With drinks in hand, elegantly dressed diners were ambling between booths looking at the possibility of purchasing the following day when the sales would be plenty. No vendor wanted to pack up merchandise for home when they could get rid of it at just above cost. Trixie found Karen pointing out a few choice pieces to a potential client.

"Busy night," Trixie commented. It was getting to the time of night when she was beginning to feel weary. It had definitely been a long day.

"Any news about Tyra Fields? When will they be charging her?" Karen clipped as she put a fallen dress back onto a padded hanger.

"Nothing yet. I have no news," Trixie shrugged. "Oh, by the way. Have you seen this woman?" Trixie pulled out the photo of Jordan dancing with Cameron Vessi.

"Oh, Cameron," Karen cooed. "The woman looks kind of familiar. Who is she?"

"She is a teacher who started right around the time you left. Her name is Jordan Jensen."

"I thought I recognized her. What was the question?" Karen seemed distracted by a woman pawing through a catalogue of sample fabrics.

"Have you seen her here in Las Vegas?" Trixie let her gaze follow Karen's to the woman pulling at a sample of fabric.

"Here? No, I haven't. Excuse me, will you?" Karen scampered off toward the distressed customer.

Trixie moved through the booths asking a few more vendors if they recognized Jordan and received negative responses. Well that seems to satisfy that. Jordan Jensen was definitely not here in Vegas. Mrs. Crawford must have been mistaken in her sighting.

The show would be starting shortly, and Trixie wanted to get a good seat. She settled in with the Minneapolis group and watched intently as two dance couples took turns performing. First, an elegant Waltz followed by a sizzling Tango. The second couple twirled out onto the floor. The woman was tiny and dressed in a sparkling barely there dress of bright yellow. Her partner was dressed conservatively in a black jump suit with a high neckline. They began with a Bolero and then finished with a fast and crisp Cha Cha. The crowd went wild standing and clapping as they bowed and then twirled off the floor. The dance music resumed inviting the audience to move out to the floor for a dance. Trixie checked the schedule for the following day. It would be the final day of competition followed by a magnificent professional competition in the evening – the culmination of the competition. She had one day to find some answers. She began to feel overwhelmed. What could she do to speed up this process? What could she do this evening?

Carl was out. She felt that sincerely. Jordan Jensen was a dead end. Mrs. Crawford was also off the suspect list. Who was left? Stephanie Sweet. Trixie sighed and pursed her lips. The last conversation with Stephanie had been disheartening. She had been distracted and overwhelmed with work. But Trixie still felt there was something Stephanie was not telling her. She had a secret, and Trixie was bound and determined to find out what that secret was. She headed toward the restaurant hoping the crowds were long gone.

She stepped in and looked around. There were few customers, and Stephanie was nowhere to be found. Maybe she was on her break. Trixie sidled up to the bar, and the bartender quickly slapped down a napkin for her order. This time she ordered a white wine. He was the same person she had spoken with when she arrived in Las Vegas. His dark good looks oozed charm, and his smile was infectious.

"You'd be a great dance teacher," she commented as he put her glass of wine carefully on her tiny napkin. He smiled revealing a set of dimples. 'I'm looking for Stephanie Sweet," she continued.

"Funny thing," he said wiping down the counter. "She went home sick. Kinda strange. She really needs the money, so it's a bit surprising for her to go home. Never happened before." He shook his head and continued to wipe down a glass mug.

Trixie frowned. It must have happened just after she showed her the photo of Jordan Jensen. Did it have to do with the photo or had she been sick and feeling poorly during their conversation? That might have something to do with her disjointed attitude.

"Do you know this woman?" Trixie whipped out the photo of Jordan Jensen.

"Sure. That's Jackie. Can't remember her last name, but she works in the casino – nights. Always shows up every morning early for a coffee – two creams – and a Rueben sandwich to take home. Why?" He was polishing another glass as he rambled about the woman in the photo.

"I showed the photo to Stephanie, and she didn't seem to recognize her," Trixie offered as she stared at the photo. "You sure this is Jackie?"

"Positive. Strange about Stephanie. She knows Jackie same as I do. I don't know why she would tell you she didn't recognize her. And I'm not sure about Jackie's last name. It starts with an H – Heidleman or Hellman. Something like that." The bartender was candid and chatty.

"How long has Jackie worked in the casino?" Trixie was betting he was mistaken at this point. No one other than Mrs. Crawford seemed to have seen the woman.

"About six months I think. She's a gymnast and trying to get into the Circe show. I think she's had a few tryouts all ready. Seems to be very determined to make it," he chattered. "She and Stephanie talk all the time about their jobs and their dates and their auditions. Everything. They're tight."

This made Trixie nervous. She now knew Stephanie had indeed left because of the photo. What did that mean? Where was she? She thanked the bartender, left him a generous tip, and headed off to the security office. They needed to know about this new development.

Trixie and the officer in charge of the investigation discussed the events of the day. Trixie related the conversation with Carl Friend. Then she explained what had happened when she showed the photo of Jordan Jensen to Stephanie Sweet and the information shared by the bartender upon her return to question Stephanie further. "Stephanie Sweet went home. I'm nervous she may be trying to run," Trixie shared. "She had a secret. I could feel it all along. I still don't know what it was, but it seems to be linked to this 'Jackie' who appears to be a look alike for Jordan Jensen."

"Are you sure it isn't indeed Jordan Jensen?" the officer asked.

"I don't think Jordan can be in two places at once, and she certainly has been in Minneapolis all this time. No, it has to be someone else," Trixie tried to remember what the bartender said was Jackie's last name. "Can we find out more about Jackie from the casino? They must have employment records with more information."

The officer grabbed the phone and put in a call for information on "Jackie". Then he made another call asking for a team to check out Stephanie Sweet's apartment. It wasn't too far away. Trixie nervously tapped her fingers on the top of the desk. She remembered she hadn't checked in with Tyra not wanting to tell her about the Jordan Jensen development.

The first call to come in was from the casino with information on Jackie Heidlemann. She had been working at the casino for about five months. Her employment records listed Minneapolis as her previous place of residence and a gymnastics gym as her former employer. Jackie worked the night shift from eleven to seven, and she was accounted for the night of Edward Garrett's murder. She was dealing black jack at the time of his death.

Trixie frowned. What did this information mean? She might have ties to Jordan Jensen – sister, cousin? She looked enough like Jordan to get a second look from Mrs. Crawford. But she certainly didn't have anything to do with the murder. Her alibi was solid. Another dead end? Trixie was perplexed by this new turn of events. She was even more perplexed when the second call came in.

The team of officers had arrived at Stephanie Sweet's apartment only to find it empty. But they passed an accident on the way to the apartment and discovered it was a pedestrian struck by a car right on Stephanie's block. After checking with the attending officers, they discovered the victim was indeed Stephanie Sweet. She was alive but in a coma at the hospital. Someone had run over their witness? There was no mistaking this coincidence! Someone was afraid Stephanie had revealed her secret. What was that secret? Trixie needed to get to the hospital. Jordan Jensen and this Jackie Heidlemann were certainly involved in this secret.

It was decided the detective would go to the casino and interview Jackie Heidlemann immediately while Trixie would go to the hospital to see Stephanie Sweet. They would also send another officer with Trixie to post at Stephanie's room. She was suddenly someone of interest in Edward Garrett's murderer. Her accident was not a coincidence. It was planned.

"After you see Miss Sweet, I want to see you back here to compare information," the detective pointed his finger squarely at Trixie. "This is becoming more than just the murder of Edward Garrett. Others are in danger. And that may include you." He stared into her eyes hoping she wouldn't take chances. He didn't need another victim.

Trixie let the officer take her arm – as if she were some sort of old lady! She hoped none of the dance crowd would see her exit the hotel door with a man in uniform. It would look bad and create some unnecessary gossip. She didn't see anyone on her way out but that didn't mean spying eyes weren't lurking behind a potted plant. The drive to the hospital was short, but she asked the officer to pull up an accident report for the incident before they arrived. She wanted as many details as possible. Stephanie Sweet was walking home to her apartment only a few

161

blocks from the hotel when she was run down from behind as she came to a corner. She wasn't even in the street or crosswalk – the driver had gone up over the curb and never stopped. Quick and efficient but not quite effective – Stephanie Sweet was still alive!

The officer ushered Trixie into the room where Stephanie laid, tubes already inserted from her body and machines monitoring her heart rate with a steady beep. She was in a coma with head injuries. The accident had occurred just after Trixie's last visit to the restaurant, so she had been in the hospital for a bit of time. She sported a cast on her leg and another on an arm. Her face showed signs of bruises beginning to emerge. Trixie dropped into the chair next to the bed and gazed on the young woman who had been so beautiful just hours before. Now she seemed pale and mummified with her casts predominantly showing,

Trixie patted her exposed hand and began to talk to her. "What secret are you still holding inside you, my dear? Why couldn't you confide in me? Was it something you couldn't share? Did someone ask you – or hire you – to approach Edward Garrett? Why? Did you have a part in this murder? What did Edward Garrett or Tyra Fields do to you?" Trixie found this attack to be very confusing. Stephanie Sweet had an alibi for the murder. So what part did she play in this whole situation?

The nurse entered and looking at the chart began to explain all of Stephanie's injuries. She explained Miss Sweet would probably stay in a

162

coma for at least a few hours but they would monitor her closely. Her injuries at this point were not life threatening although they were serious. Trixie asked they restrict her visitors and said there would be an officer on duty outside her door as this was not an accident. It was indeed deliberate. The nurse raised an eyebrow but didn't question anything Trixie told her.

Trixie went back to the hotel debating what to do next. She knew she should check in with Tyra, but should she mention this latest development? She must. It was a crucial piece of the puzzle. But how? Maybe Tyra would have a clue. First, she would check in with security to find what the interview with Jackie had uncovered.

The interview, Trixie discovered, had been non-existent. In fact Jackie had also left her job with a strange sickness just as Stephanie had. Stephanie Sweet had stopped in at the casino just before Jackie suddenly came down with her illness. And just as with Stephanie, Jackie never made it home. Her husband had become quite concerned when police showed up looking for her. They had put out an all points bulletin for her car, but so far nothing had turned up yet. Trixie began to worry about Jackie just as she worried about Stephanie.

Trixie slowly made her way to Tyra Fields room. She felt heaviness inside her – two women hurt or missing. What was this all about? How did these women fit in with the murder of Edward Garrett? Tyra was sprawled out on the bed with a romantic movie on the TV. The hotel had brought her dinner that sat half eaten on the tray in the corner. She nursed a drink in one hand and had a box of tissues plopped on her lap for the sad parts of the story. A few crumpled wads of tissue were already strewn across the bed. "Well?" she blurted out when Trixie settled herself into the chair by the bed.

Trixie proceeded to explain the whole Jackie/Jordan Jensen mess. Tyra quickly flipped off the TV as Trixie explained Mrs. Crawford's spotting of Jordan in Las Vegas only to discover it was actually a sister or relative named Jackie. She got to the part about showing the photo of Jordan to Stephanie Sweet, her visit to Jackie, and hit and run accident. "So Stephanie is in a coma in the hospital with a police guard at her door, and Jackie is nowhere to be found."

"What do you mean she is nowhere to be found?" Tyra's voice became agitated.

"She also went home sick but never made it. The police are on the lookout for her car, but so far no luck."

"What do you think that means?" Tyra's eyes became wide as she gulped her drink.

"Well, either she is also the victim of foul play as was Stephanie, or she caused the foul play. They were both involved somehow. I can't tell you how. I can't tell you why." Trixie shrugged her shoulders and began to ponder all the pieces but nothing made sense. Neither one was the murderer of Edward Garrett. Both had been working – verified alibis. So how did they fit into this whole mess?

XV.

"We have one day left," Trixie leaned forward as she discussed these last developments with the policeman in charge of the investigation. It was late, and he sipped a black coffee.

"So we have two people who shouldn't be involved but are, and lots of people who should be involved but aren't?" He frowned at the list Trixie had shoved in front of him with names and comments.

"You got it. Any news about Jackie Heidlemann?" Trixie pointed to the top name on the list.

"Nope. And we're beginning to become a bit concerned because her husband swears she knows nothing about the murder and has never mentioned the name Edward Garrett."

"I suggest you have someone from the Minneapolis department interview Jordan Jensen about this Jackie. Then I think we need to talk with the kitchen staff about locating Luz Maria. We need to find her to identify the woman she saw. I hope she isn't another victim. My guess is

165

she is an illegal alien who went into hiding so as not to be discovered," Trixie outlined her suggestions. "And I think we need to think about letting Tyra Fields out of her room."

The detective stared at Trixie. "And why would we do that? It's dangerous for her."

"Exactly. We need to flush out the killer. Jackie and Stephanie did not kill Edward Garrett. Either they know who did, or they are somehow involved in some other way. But they did not murder Edward. There is a third party. That person will only make a mistake if Tyra is released. Right now that person thinks they are safe because Tyra Fields is the suspect in custody."

The detective pursed his lips and let his finger go down Trixie's list again. So who was the murderer?

Trixie accompanied the detective down to the kitchen. The same supervisor Trixie had used for translation with Luz Maria was working. He tried to appear as if he were too busy for conversation, but the badge the detective flashed got his attention, and he finally agreed to take a break for a little discussion. The three sat around a bare round table in the corner of the break room. The man was clearly nervous as he chewed on his lower lip. His eyes remained glued to the top of the table.

166

In perfect Spanish, the detective explained they were not interested in arresting Luz Maria for illegal entry into the United States, but only needed her help in solving a murder. He made it clear if she cooperated, she might be granted a green card. The supervisor twisted his mouth as the detective spoke quickly again and again reinforcing their need for her help. Trixie prayed the promises were believable. She knew Luz Maria was their best source to solve this murder.

Finally, the supervisor nodded. Luz Maria was indeed hiding, and he could contact her. The promise of a green card might bring her back for a meeting. They agreed to meet the next morning behind the hotel in the parking lot if the detective promised to come alone.

Trixie and the policeman discussed the developments before they called it a night. It was late and decisions would have to be made tomorrow. It was their last chance, and both knew tomorrow would be crucial in solving this murder.

Settled in her bed, Trixie was awakened by a quiet rap on her door. Had she imagined it? No, there it was again. Another light rap. Wrapping herself in a blanket, she peered out the peep hole and spotted the top of a head. She opened the door to Luz Maria and a young girl. They scurried in, and Trixie quickly shut the door.

The girl spoke, translating. "My mother does not trust the policia. She will speak to you but does not speak any English. I will translate for

167

her." The girl was about ten or eleven but seemed very mature – possibly a frequent translator for Luz Maria. She was dressed in clean black jeans and a t-shirt with a photo of a dog on the front. Her sleek black hair was pulled back into a neat ponytail. Extending her hand she introduced herself, "I'm her daughter, Anita."

They sat down in the chairs, and Trixie took the edge of the bed. Trixie pondered what questions to ask. She had a sudden burst of energy as she sat across from the tiny woman with the soft eyes. She sighed deeply and began by explaining the man who was murdered was her boss and friend. Luz Maria's eyes widened. She nodded her understanding without the help of her translator.

"Can your mother describe the woman who took the meal cart from her that night?" Trixie listened for the translation. Luz Maria at first looked puzzled as if she was trying to think carefully back to that night.

"How tall was she? Taller than me?" Trixie stood up, and Luz Maria stood up to compare.

Luz Maria let go a lengthy spew of Spanish using her hands to explain. Anita turned to Trixie. "She said she was about your height. Not too tall but taller than she is. She was thin and wearing all black."

Trixie frowned. "Was she wearing pants or a skirt?" She motioned with her own hands indicating a flowing skirt or long pants. Then she played with her hair. "Hair color?"

Anita said, "Pantalones? Falda? Pela?" Luz Maria began a detailed explanation with lots of hand motions. Anita turned to Trixie. "Her hair was covered by a scarf so she doesn't know what color hair. She was wearing a black skirt and a black shawl over a black blouse or shirt."

"Hmmm. So very generic. Not much help." Trixie sighed. No better than she was this afternoon.

Luz Maria could see the disappointment in Trixie's face and voice. She may have experienced the death of a relative or friend herself, and her eyes saddened. Then she began to speak again. Anita listened carefully and turned toward Trixie to translate. "She says she is sorry. She is sorry you have lost your friend. The woman didn't wear anything unusual but she did look older – like about her own age – and she had a ring on her finger. It was very beautiful. Does that help?"

Trixie smiled and thanked the two. "Yes," she nodded. "That is a big help. Tell your mother I will make sure she gets her green card for all of her help."

Both smiled. There was no need for translation.

When they left, she called security and asked for the detective in charge of the murder. They patched through her call to his cell phone so she could relate the conversation with her visitors. Even through the phone she could tell he was disappointed he didn't get the chance to meet personally with Luz Maria but said he would follow up on the promise to get the woman her green card. "We found Jackie's car. It was abandoned about a hundred miles east of Las Vegas. It doesn't look like foul play was involved. She may have caught a ride with a passing motorist. But we will keep looking in case she was abducted. Minneapolis police spoke with Jordan Jensen and discovered Jackie is her twin sister. She was unaware of any connection between Jackie and Edward's death. In fact, she said she hadn't heard from her sister in a few weeks. So the news of her disappearance was quite shocking. I don't know if she was truthful, but we're checking her phone records for any calls from her sister."

All leads seemed to dead-end. Their only hope was either Stephanie coming out of her coma to give them further information on her connection to the murder or the flushing out of the person with the announcement of Tyra Field's release and innocence. Would either of these tactics work? They had a day to find out.

XVI.

Trixie rose early and headed down to the security office. The detective was already in his office looking tired and worn. He nursed a large black coffee in one hand and was writing on a large board with the other.

"What's this?" Trixie took a chair and glanced at the board.

"A time line," he muttered continuing to write. At the top of the board was a time frame of the day Edward Garrett was killed. The detective began to explain from the first point down. "Someone stole Tyra Fields' room key before the call from her suite for room service at 2:30 in the afternoon. That person had to have knowledge of Tyra's room number and her bag in order to snatch that key. But, they didn't know Edward Garrett very well because they didn't know he would not order a steak dinner."

"However," Trixie added, "they needed to order something with a sharp knife for the murder weapon to be on that tray. And they also needed to know Edward's room number."

The detective raised his pen in acknowledgement of these points and added them to the chart. "We know the caller could not have been Stephanie Sweet because she was at the competition with Edward Garrett watching Tyra and Tino competing." Trixie nodded. He continued, "We

171

also know that the murderer was not Stephanie nor was it Jackie because they were both working when the murder took place at approximately 1:30 am. But the murderer had to have been someone Edward knew because he let that person in. We also know that person was, according to Luz Maria, a woman."

"We know that woman wasn't Jordan Jensen because she couldn't have been both here and in Minneapolis. The flight records have no one by that name or description flying between Minneapolis and Las Vegas before or after the murder. We also know the murder was committed to incriminate Tyra Fields. The murder of Edward Garrett appears to have had nothing directly to do with Edward himself. The murderer took the knife after murdering Edward Garrett and using Tyra's key card, put the weapon in her bathroom wastebasket. That was quite bold considering Tyra might have been in the room at the time. Clearly the murderer did not know Tyra had an air tight alibi for the time of the murder. Then the murderer called in the tip about the knife from a hotel phone probably in the lobby or casino — someplace we wouldn't be able to trace." The detective pursed his lips in thought then continued. "We know both Stephanie and Jackie were somehow involved because right after you showed Stephanie Jordan's photo, she suddenly got ill and left work. Jackie, Jordan's twin sister left work as well. Stephanie Sweet's accident was deliberate. She was purposely run down for something she knew or saw. Then Jackie disappeared — she's either kidnapped or on the run.

We need to find Jackie because Stephanie is right now in no condition to provide any information. One or both of these women have some of the answers to our puzzle."

Trixie nodded her agreement. "We need to announce to the competitors that Tyra Fields and Tino Van Arp will be performing tonight with the rest of the professional top winners in this evening's show. We need to flush out the person responsible for this chaos — the third person — the murderer." The detective pondered. It was dangerous but necessary. He was considering how best to provide protection for Tyra Fields during this daring maneuver. His personnel would have to be undercover — dressed like dancers. That could be a problem. He thought about his officers and debated how to pull off that little charade. A tux did not a dancer make. He chuckled at the thought of this charade.

Trixie gave him some suggestions on attire and decided to get some breakfast before this trying and busy day. Her stomach was growling uncontrollably. She ambled down to the restaurant half expecting to see Stephanie working yet knowing she was indeed lying in a bed in the local hospital with tubes coming out of her. Settling onto a seat at the counter, she waved to the bartender she had spoken to several times now, and he brought her a steaming cup of coffee and a menu. Ordering a breakfast special with pancakes and eggs, she settled back to sip her coffee and consider what to tell Tyra and Tino.

The bartender refilled her cup and asked her if she had seen Stephanie. By now the news of her accident had spread through the restaurant staff. Trixie nodded then asked a question. "You hear lots of things working here," she began. "Were Jackie and Stephanie good friends?"

"Yeah, you might say they were fairly close. Which reminds me, Jackie didn't stop in for her coffee and sandwich yet." His face showed a puzzled expression.

"Jackie is missing," Trixie informed him without giving details. He stepped back holding the coffee pot and waited for more details. Instead, Trixie asked him another question. "Was there anyone else you noticed asking to speak with Stephanie? Other than the murder victim, Edward Garrett, was there anyone from the dance competition who spoke specifically with Stephanie for any reason?"

The bartender put the pot down and thought for a moment. "Well, there was someone who came in and had breakfast with Jackie recently. I think Stephanie was probably the server." He pointed over to one of the corner booths. "They sat right over there. It was one morning right after Jackie came in for her usual coffee and sandwich."

"Who was it? Do you know?" Trixie began to feel a heightened sense of excitement at this tidbit of information. Reaching into her purse, she pulled out some of the photos she had used to compare Jordan

174

Jensen's photo earlier. There were a couple pictures of the studio back in Minneapolis and a few of the staff as well as the students. She pushed them across the counter. "Anyone in these photos? Do you recognize someone here as the person who met with Jackie?"

The bartender studied the pictures and tilting his head a bit pointed to one. "Yes, this seems to be the person right here. The hair is bit different, but I think that is the person who met with Jackie." Trixie stared at the one he was pointing to and sucked in a breath. Not who she had expected. Not at all. She eagerly ate her breakfast while she dialed the detective and finished the last sip of her coffee before calling Tyra. "I'm coming to your room shortly," she relayed and hung up quickly. She knew not to say too much in public.

When she reached the security office, she noticed she had missed a call. It was from the studio and had come through late last night. It was early in Minneapolis so no one would be in the studio just yet, but thinking it might be important, she dialed Ashley Arthur's home phone number.

"Hello," came the sleepy response.

"Ashley, did you call me last night? This is Trixie," she began only to be interrupted by a tirade of words from a no longer tired Ashley Arthur.

"Oh, my goodness! Oh, my goodness!" he began repeating the phrase over and over again. "The police came to the studio as we were closing up and took Jordan into custody. Yes, I said into custody with her hands handcuffed behind her back and everything. I guess her sister Jackie was also arrested. Now today I have to cancel her appointments until they call with information on what is happening. I'm freaking out! Oh, my goodness!"

Trixie frowned at his breathy explanation and told him to calm down. She would find out what to do about this situation and get back with him later. "Just cancel the appointments and don't worry," she begged trying to sooth his concerns.

Turning to the detective, she noticed he was on the phone as well. What a mess. At least she knew Jackie was safe and not in danger . . . at least that was what she assumed. The detective got off the phone and leaned back in his chair to ponder the developments.

"My staff just told me Jordan and Jackie have been arrested," she quipped. "And I have some information from the restaurant bartender about our third person."

Looking tired and drained, the detective focused his attentions on Trixie and her new information. "It's not what I would have guessed," she began explaining her conversation this morning during breakfast. "How is Stephanie Sweet? Any improvement?"

He shook his head and took another moment to think. "It's time to release Tyra Fields," he said with a flat tone to his voice.

"It might put her in danger without some security measures. After all, the media and people here in the hotel and at the dance event think she is a murderer," Trixie reminded him. "I know it is our only solution, but we need to review her safety as well."

"I'm aware of that," he said. "We won't give out any new information about her release to the press until after she is announced as a performer tonight in the professional show. We owe her that much." Trixie agreed and said she would inform Tyra and Tino about the announcement. She made up her mind not to mention the arrest of Jordan Jensen and her twin sister Jackie when she spoke with Tyra. It could make the situation a bit tense. After all, Tyra would find out all the details later.

Trixie left the security office and made her way to the ballroom. The competition was in full swing with finals for many of the pro/am divisions on this final day of dancing. Tino Van Arp was standing on the sidelines waiting to take his place on the floor with a nervous student. She was pacing a bit and smiling back at the crowd of Minneapolis students up early to watch her performance. There were pockets of dancers clustered around the floor; some were in costume and others were sipping tall cups of gourmet coffees. The music was beating loudly for the current group of competitors.

Trixie decided to wait until after the next performance to talk with Tino about this evening's show. She meandered back into the vendors display room. With this the last day, the booth owners and workers were busily trying to unload as much merchandise as possible to make this trip worthwhile and eliminate some of the tedious packing required later tonight. Many of the competitors had waited for this day to make purchases hoping for better discounts on the prices. One jewelry owner was haggling with a woman about the price of a necklace, and Karen Danbury had a tape measure draped around her neck as she took measurements for a dress order. Several dancers were trying on pairs of dance shoes with the boxes scattered across the floor. It was a buzz of activity back here.

Trixie peeked out to the dance floor to watch a bit of Tino's performance. He was dancing well as was his student. She deserved high marks and would most likely place very well. When winners were announced they were recorded on the computer and a print out of placements were posted on the stands at the entry to the ballrooms. Trixie took a few minutes to check the list for her Minneapolis students and nodded her approval at several excellent performances. For a moment she forgot about the reason for her own presence in Las Vegas. For a moment she forgot that Edward Garrett had been murdered. She forgot that her time the past few days had been consumed with doubts about friends and co-workers in the search for a murderer. But tonight it would all be over. Tonight they would know the truth about this whole sorted situation. At least that was what she hoped would happen. If not, the trip home would be a nightmare. Speaking of the trip home, she reminded herself she had no ticket back to the Twin Cities yet and would have to stop in at the travel agency to see what was available. Things in her schedule just hadn't progressed to the point of finding her way home. She sighed and glanced back to see Tino and his student walk off the floor with bright smiles and hopeful success.

Scurrying back into the ballroom, she grabbed Tino's elbow and guided him out to the hallway for a private conversation. "You and Tyra will be performing tonight in the professional show," she announced brightly expecting him to react with excited glee. Instead he frowned and shook his head. "What's wrong? I thought you'd be thrilled," she questioned.

"We haven't practiced at all. We need to get together before tonight, that's all. Can you tell me where she is so we can arrange some time to go over routines?" Tino spread his hands in a pleading manner.

"Listen, we can't have Tyra walking around the competition until you two hit the floor. With all the media attention to her as the murderer, she is in a questionable situation here. And you certainly can't tell anyone about this – not until it is formally announced tonight just before you walk out onto that floor. Do you understand me?" She tried her best to explain the grave situation they were facing. She didn't mention the possibility of there being several people involved in this murder scheme. She needed to keep this part a secret even from Tino. She could tell by his expression he hadn't understood what she was trying to tell him. He was only interested in their dance performance. Ok, so maybe she would take him to see Tyra but just for a moment to two. "I can take you with me in a couple of minutes to meet with Tyra if you'd like," she offered finally after a short debate with herself on safety. He smiled and nodded. "Meet me in the lobby in a half hour or so," she continued glancing at her watch. That would give her enough time to find a flight home.

There was one seat left on the redeye leaving at one am in the morning. She snatched it up hoping things would be well on their way to a solution by that time. She wondered how long Stephanie would be in her coma. Should she take the time this afternoon to visit her again in the hospital? It couldn't hurt. Or maybe it could – someone might think she was getting some vital piece of evidence. No one knew Stephanie Sweet's condition. That was to remain secure.

Trixie called Tyra and told her she was bringing Tino for a short visit. She spotted Tino leaning on a table in the lobby as he tried to scan the headlines of the newspaper spread out across the glossy tabletop and after a quick glance around the area deemed it safe to take him to the locked door beyond the elevators where Tyra was waiting for their knock. Tino laughed as they passed the construction zone. "So this is where you've been holing up the past few days," he chuckled. "I thought you were actually in solitary confinement!" Glancing around the room at the bed and TV he nodded. "Well, maybe you were in solitary after all."

Trixie sat them down and began to explain what would occur this evening. She paced back and forth as she spoke. "You both will be performing for the professional show, but there will be no announcement until just before you head out on that floor. We want no media coverage of the released murderess or anything like that. We want you both to be secure and safe, so no mention of this to anyone. . . and I mean anyone!" she emphasized in a slow strong voice. "Got me?" They both nodded. She didn't want to explain the whole thing to them. She didn't want to tell them about the situation back in Minneapolis with Jordan and Jackie in custody, nor did she want to tell them Stephanie Sweet was still in serious condition after being struck deliberately by a hit and run driver. They could find out later all the details of the past few days. Right now they needed to understand the danger their public appearance could bring if anyone found out before time.

Tyra seemed upbeat by the news. She was itching to get back to performing. Sliding off her seat on the bed she pulled out a bag from the closet. "I have a new dress for the performance," she announced gleefully.

Tino groaned. "But we haven't practiced with a new outfit. How do we know how our moves will work? What if there are problems?"

Tyra only grinned. Abruptly turning toward Trixie, she tossed a hand through her hair and asked if Trixie would get her a bottle of hair dye. "I need a new look", she announced. "I think I'll go dark. Black!" Her eyes glistened with renewed excitement.

"Well, that should confuse people enough to keep you a bit more secure," Trixie agreed. "Where did you get this dress?" She fingered the canary yellow two piece outfit edged in fringe and stones.

"I picked it up when I first arrived from Karen's inventory. The black hair color will really set off this color, don't you think?" Tyra held up the short skirt and gave it a quick shake to show the sparkle. Her thin lips turned up into a smile.

Tino groaned again. "Let's try a few warm ups. There is a little room in the hallway." He took Tyra's hand and spun her out into the open space to lead a few steps. Trixie stayed in the room and slid her hand along the fabric of the new dress. How much did this little number cost? It had to be from the gently used dress rack — there was not enough time for Tyra to order a custom made gown. Dance couples frequently wore matching outfits for one dance season and then commissioned designers like Karen to resell their costumes giving them cash for new custom designs. It saved on cost not only for the resellers but for the new owners who purchased at a discount. The designers also received a sales commission as well as a new order from the selling couple.

XVII.

Trixie decided to take a walk to the hospital for a check in on Stephanie Sweet. It would also give her a chance to pick up hair dye. She didn't want anyone from the competition to notice her purchase. It might raise some questions. Stephanie was still in a coma with an armed guard at the door, so Trixie decided to just chat with the officer seated in front of her door.

"Has anyone come to visit Stephanie?" She showed her identification and introduced herself. Evidently there was a list of acceptable visitors, and her name was indeed on the list. She welcomed the additional security measures. The officer shook his head. No one other than police and doctors had visited Stephanie. Trixie felt a wave of relief. At least for the moment. Would someone try to finish the job or were they so confident in Tyra's arrest and subsequent conviction they would let the matter go? After all, tonight it would most assuredly be over with the competition dancers leaving Las Vegas for good.

Finding a drug store was easy. There were several possibilities along her route back to the hotel. She located a shelf loaded with hair color and selected one with added conditioner and natural highlights. With Tyra's bleached blond hair, this hair color needed to be the best possible. She paid for her purchase and tucked the bag into her purse. Then she called Tyra to let her know she had the black dye. Tyra seemed delighted at the news. She and Tino had practiced for a good hour before he had escaped again through the locked door between occupied hotel and demolition zone. Tyra was once again alone and anxious to prepare for the evening's show.

Trixie dropped off her package wondering what changes would take place in Tyra's appearance over the course of the next few hours. Trixie pondered the plan for the evening. She pursed her lips and prayed for success. Too many people had already been murdered or injured already — first, Edward Garrett and then Stephanie Sweet. She prayed no one else would fall into similar dire situations.

The afternoon would be boring — a tedious waiting game. Trixie decided to settle in at the restaurant for a sandwich. She settled into her favorite stool at the counter as her favorite bartender slapped down the menu in front of her and began to pour a glass of white wine with a smirk.

"I didn't order this," Trixie protested as he set the glass in front of her.

"Someday you'll let me make you a real drink. Maybe one of my specialties," he grinned. "Any news about Stephanie?" His face suddenly became concerned.

"You are very fond of Stephanie, aren't you," Trixie tilted her head with sudden recognition of the affection in his face. He turned away from her quickly pretending to stack glasses but his neck turned an embarrassed pick color. "No, to answer your question. There hasn't been any further news about Stephanie's condition." Trixie paused for a moment staring at the menu items. "I'll take a Ruben sandwich with a side salad." She passed the menu toward the edge of the counter and asked, "Have you told her how you feel?"

The bartender turned slowly and shook his head. "I'm just a lowly bartender. Why would Stephanie notice me? With all of these rich high rollers, why would Stephanie Sweet see any future in me?"

"Don't sell yourself short. You've got exactly what all those high rollers would pay big bucks for." Trixie waited for the bartender to whirl around and stare back.

"And what would that be?" He frowned as he picked up the menu and slipped it back into its slot behind the counter.

"Besides talent — I understand you make a mean drink, you have good looks and youth. We never appreciate that until it's long gone. You may not believe this, but at one time I was considered a beauty!" Trixie touched her hair and tossed her head smiling like a Miss America contestant.

The bartender laughed throwing his head back. "I guess you are right. I am a pretty talented and creative fellow. And yes, I am young I guess. At least compared to the regular customers we get," he tossed his head toward a couple of dancers sauntering by in their competition attire. The gentleman was balding and hunched as he walked. The wife was tiny and birdlike with a wrinkled complexion covered in dark foundation with heavy rosy rouge on her cheeks. She was grasping onto his arm for support as she wobbled on high heeled dance shoes.

Trixie waited for her sandwich and lifted her glass to her lips as she wondered how it would feel to be young again. "You have no idea how much someone would pay to be in your shoes and able to redo what they already screwed up in a past life. You are a luck man. Now just take the plunge and tell Stephanie Sweet how sweet she really is," Trixie advised thinking about the poor woman lying in a hospital bed — a woman who needed a man like this.

The sandwich came out thick and delicious with a wooden bowl of tossed salad topped with dressing and croutons. Trixie suddenly felt very hungry. She grasped one half of the thick breaded sandwich and took a mouth watering bite. "I don't know how late you work today, but take my

186

advice. Come to the show tonight in the ballroom. I think you'll see a real show! Can't say anything more," Trixie raised an eyebrow peaking the bartender's curiosity.

Trixie sat in her room with the television blaring staring at her one black dress hanging ready to wear again. When this week was over, she vowed to burn that dress. She carefully combed her hair into place and pulled out what little make up she had to reapply another layer. There had been a time with applying this color had been a pleasure — something to enhance her beauty. Now it was a way to hide her aging paleness and to add emphasis to her best features. Just were those features? She stared into the mirror trying to locate something she found to be pleasing. Today she was having more difficulty than usual. "You, Trixie Appleby have inner beauty!" she pronounced with a sparkle in her voice.

After watching a few reruns of Andy Griffith, Trixie called Tyra to tell her she would be over shortly. But first, she had an errand. She needed to speak with the event coordinator about Tyra and Tino's appearance in tonight's show. There were a few competitions still in progress but the majority of the competitors and audience were off getting ready for the evening's event. Trixie spotted Carl Friend on the floor judging the remaining contestants along with the other judges. He paid no attention to her appearance in the ballroom gazing instead at the couple performing the Samba directly in front of him.

Trixie glanced around the room finally locating Barry Whittley at the tabulation table in the front of the room. She sidled around the room until she reached the table and motion to get Barry's attention. He smiled back and excused himself to join her in a deserted corner of the ballroom.

"Barry," Trixie began. "Tyra Fields and Tino Van Arp will be performing tonight along with the other champions."

"But I thought.. ." Barry began in a harsh whisper.

"I know, I know. You thought Tyra was arrested for Edward's murder. Well she had an air tight alibi and has been in protective custody. Which is why it is imperative that no one else knows about this but you and me," she glared directly into his eyes and motioned with her finger between the two of them. "Imperative," she repeated.

"There could be serious repercussions if Tyra Fields shows up tonight," Barry frowned as if in deep thought. "Serious repercussions!"

"Exactly, Barry. So please do me this great favor and keep this strictly between us. Don't mention this to anyone. And I mean anyone," Trixie looked beyond Barry's gaping mouth toward Carl Friend standing along the sidelines of the dance floor. Carl would be in shock with Tyra's appearance, she was sure. There would be many in shock when Tyra Fields' name was announced this evening. Trixie breathed deeply as she gazed around the room very quiet and calm at the moment. That would change.

After leaving Barry, Trixie rapped on the secret door and slipped in as it opened a crack. Tyra was transformed from a blond scarecrow to a dark haired exotic beauty. Her newly dyed hair was a sleek black pulled back from her classic face into a stylish up-do. Her spray on tan and creamy foundation completely hid the freckled skin tones Tyra usually sported. In addition to the vibrant red lipstick outlining her normally thin lips, her eyes were coated in black liner and flecked with sparkling shadow. Filmy false eyelashes fluttered like huge butterfly wings drawing attention to her smoldering smoky eyes. Dressed in her new two piece yellow costume, Tyra's model thin body successfully showed off the glittery design of the stoned top and clingy skirt. The skirt wrapped around her slender hips like a tourniquet with layers of fringe dripping below. Tyra stood in front of the mirror and shook her body making the fringe swirl out away from her body like a hip shaking hula dancer. Flesh colored fishnets clung to her pencil thin legs. Fishnets were an integral part of a competition dancer's uniform. Her nude strappy Latin heels made her legs look miles long. Trixie recalled the days many years ago when she dared wear three inch heels like the ones Tyra sported today. Oh, to be young again.

"Well, what do you think?" Tyra Fields spun around and struck a pose. Trixie just nodded her approval.

189

"Remember, you need to be careful," Trixie warned. Tyra glared at her over her shoulder. She didn't look worried. Trixie thought this might be a mistake — a big mistake.

Grabbing a dance jacket designed like a high school letter jacket, Tyra announced she was ready to go. Her jacket in black satin sported a dance logo on the back in colorful threading. Would she be unrecognizable as they scurried to the ballroom? Trixie reminded her they would have a bodyguard in the hallways but once she and Tino hit the dance floor, she would be on her own. Tyra gave her a roll of her eyes. They proceeded out the door toward a burly black suited man with a crew cut flashing his badge in their direction.

Tino Van Arp stood by the ballroom doorway waiting. He shifted his weight nervously from foot to foot shaking out his legs in preparation. He wore a slim black jumpsuit with a plunging V in the front. His black dance shoes sported the higher Cuban heel giving his slender build a taller appearance. He was equal in height to Tyra and this could give a well balanced coupling. Tyra's newly black hair gave the pair a similar appearance as well. Some judges preferred this similar look for dance partners.

As Tino and Tyra waited at the door, Trixie walked into the ballroom and scanned the room for Barry. She kept her eye open for security. Would she recognize anyone? Would they stand out or had they managed to dress appropriately for a dance competition? No one stood out. Everything appeared to be quite normal. She hoped the bodyguard for Tyra was ready for action if something were to happen. Trixie's mind stopped cold. It wasn't "if something were to happen" but when something happened. She was sure Tyra's appearance tonight would cause quite a stir. She spotted Barry and managed to move around the crowds until she was standing right next to him. He ignored her for a moment or two nodding to one of the volunteers making arrangements between the dancers and those playing the music. He was listening intently and nodding as he glanced toward Trixie. She gave him a gesture that all was set to go. Barry seemed to understand quite clearly what was about to happen. The room was filled with competitors and guests with all the tables around the dance floor filled and large numbers standing around the doorways between the hallway and the ballroom as well as between the vendor spaces. One championship couple had just performed and there was a din of conversation filling the room before the next exhibition.

Barry Whittley moved up to the microphone and thanked the previous couple for their stunning performance. Then he paused briefly as if choosing his words carefully. "And now please welcome our next exhibition. From Minneapolis, Minnesota please welcome to the floor Tyra Fields and her partner Tino Van Arp dancing a Latin medley." The crowd gasped as the pair pranced to the dance floor. Tyra's yellow top picked up the lights from above giving a glittery shimmer. She shook her hips and the fringe swung freely as she took her place in the center of the floor. Tino stood boldly behind her in a masculine stance waiting for the music to begin.

Trixie glanced around the room waiting. She found Carl Friend standing on the opposite side of the room. He was leaning casually against the wall glaring at the couple on the floor. Mrs. Crawford was seated at a table facing the floor. Her hand was clasped to her mouth and her eyes were wildly staring at the newly dark haired woman ready to begin dancing. Barry Whittley grasped Trixie's elbow and frowned. He was nervous, waiting, anticipating.

In the doorway stood the bartender. He had been curious enough to come see what Trixie was referring to in their earlier conversation. He caught Trixie's eye and nodded then continued to look around the room for anything out of the ordinary as was Trixie. Only a minute had passed since Tyra and Tino had taken the floor but it seemed time was in slow motion. Finally the music began with a roll of the percussion, and the pair began to move.

The music seemed to drown out any background commotion so Trixie let her eyes dart from corner to corner trying to notice anything abnormal. But what was abnormal? She didn't quite know what she was looking to see. Her chest began to heave with deep breathing. She could feel her heart pounding. Suddenly from the right corner came movement.

192

Not just movement, but quick movement. Trixie expected some to guests to meander during the routine, but this movement seemed fast like someone running. In a flash, a body seemed to hurl past the groups of people huddled in areas for gossip and comments about this sudden appearance of an apparent murderer. Racing after the person in motion was a waiter dressed in a black tuxedo. Was this an undercover cop waiting just as she was? The person running through the crowds suddenly pulled up and standing against the doorway for that little bit of additional light streaming through from the hallway lifted their arms revealing a glint of a gun. The pursuing waiter wasn't yet to the doorway and was in fact waylaid by people craning their necks for a better look at the mayhem. Trixie's heart began to flutter as she watched in slow motion the arm lift, gun in hand and point toward the spinning Tyra Fields out on the floor with no notion of the danger about to cut short her life. Suddenly from behind, a body tackled the shooter with a crashing motion causing the gun to spin across the wooden dance floor to the gasps of the crowd.

Tyra Fields stopped dancing, standing frozen in the center of the floor until Tino wrapped her up into his arms and rushed her toward the protection of the scoring table. Trixie standing on tiptoes managed to spot the tackler as he stood up. It was the bartender in the thick of the action. The waiter with backup from the bodyguard quickly grabbed the shooter shrouded in a black hooded cape. The head covering slipped off revealing Karen Danbury sputtering after the flying hit from the bartender. She was gasping for air as the larger men pulled her arms behind her back. Her gray streaked hair was damp with perspiration, and she grimaced not from pain but from anger.

As Karen was escorted out of the ballroom, Barry Whittley invited Tyra and Tino to complete their performance. His voice was calm and settling as the whispers and conversation died down returning the dancers to their seats. Most had no idea what had just occurred, but the gossip would continue to spread throughout the evening.

Tino and Tyra returned to the floor to begin their routine once again. At first Tyra seemed unsteady and shaken, but as the music continued to play she began to relax and feel the pulse of the music move her from combination to combination with a new energy. It must have just settled in that her journey was indeed over — she was no longer the suspect. She was now the innocent. The audience sensed the same and gave the pair a standing ovation when they completed the performance and took their bow.

"What just happened?" Trixie asked when she found the detective back in the security office. "And where were you?" she demanded.

"We had Karen Danbury in our sights as the introduction of Tyra Fields was made in the ballroom. We waited to see what her reaction would be. We expected surprise and shock. We didn't expect her to grab a gun and race out to the ballroom to finish the job," his face was stoic as he recalled what happened.

"I thought you would have more men scattered around the room and not just one lone waiter!" She tilted her head and waited for an explanation.

"We did! But they were watching the other suspects and nowhere near the shooter. We were lucky Luke happened to be standing behind Ms. Danbury when she decided to take her stand." He breathed out with a sigh.

"Luke? Is he the bartender? Does he work for you?" Trixie leaned forward in her chair.

"Yes, he is the bartender. And no, he doesn't work for us. But I'd love to have him on our team. He is a personable hardworking young man as far as I can tell," he noted.

Trixie smiled. There could be a change in Luke's future. He could be using his other talents in a most productive way. "Any news about Stephanie Sweet's condition?"

"Actually, we just received a call from the hospital that she came out of her coma this afternoon. I'm going over there right now. Want to join me?" He stood and waited for a reply.

Checking her watch, Trixie nodded. Just because they had nabbed the murderer doesn't mean there were not questions to be answered. "And why did Karen Danbury kill Edward Garrett?" Trixie asked her questions as they walked toward the hospital. It was a pleasant evening, and this was the first time it felt really good to take this walk.

"At first she denied everything and wouldn't say a word. Then she broke down and admitted her involvement. She claims it was due to Cameron Vessi. Karen blamed Tyra for stealing her dance partner — her future and only opportunity to actually do something personally with her dancing." Trixie nodded at the explanation. She knew Karen was feeling her age and wanted to have one last feather in her cap before hanging up her dance shoes, but with Tyra's interest in Cameron, that dream quickly ended forever.

The detective continued. "She ranted and raved pretty good calling Miss Tyra every name in the book. I guess there was no love there. But Karen did love Cameron. Oh, not as a romantic interest because she truly loves her husband, but she loved him as a human being. She believed Tyra was the cause of his early death. She couldn't stand the screaming and fighting between them and blamed it all on Tyra Fields. So when she spotted Jackie, the twin sister of Jordon Jensen who was the one time love of Cameron Vessi, Karen hatched a plan to take revenge on the person she felt was responsible for all of her pain. It triggered those old feelings again to see someone from the past. Jackie reminded her of what she had lost." The detective was suddenly quiet.

"And Stephanie Sweet?" Trixie hoped Stephanie wasn't involved. She hoped she was an innocent — for Luke's sake.

196

"We don't know. All we know is Stephanie was run down. We don't know why at this point or who might have done the deed."

The hospital was quiet when they arrived, but the guard was still stationed at Stephanie Sweet's door. With a nod, they entered to see a woman sitting up rather than lying listlessly. The tubes had been removed, and she appeared haggard but alive. Her eyes widened with fear as Trixie took a seat along side of the bed. The detective introduced himself and flashed his badge. Her eyes lowered, and she let out a deep sigh.

"Miss Sweet," he began. "We've caught Karen Danbury and will be charging her with the murder of Edward Garrett." He waited for a reaction from Stephanie. It was no longer fear but relief that appeared on her face. "Can you tell me how you were involved?"

"Oh, my." There was hesitation before Stephanie started her story. "My friend Jackie brought Karen in for breakfast one morning, and I was their server. I heard them discuss a plan to implicate someone they both knew in an embarrassing situation. I didn't know who exactly the victim was nor who they planned to blame. But they asked if I would simply get to know a man from the dance competition. You know. Just keep him busy for the evening so they could put their plan into place. I didn't see any harm in that. The person they wanted blamed was someone who had destroyed some lives — people the two of them loved and held dear. It was a sad story. I've known people like that. People who don't care who they hurt. They never seem to get their own dreams dashed to pieces after they've demolished someone else. I know how that is. So I introduced myself to Edward and found him to be charming. I really enjoyed my evening with Mr. Garrett. So it was quite shocking to find him dead. I had no idea murder was part of their plan. No idea!" Stephanie shook her head. "I didn't want to believe Jackie and Karen were involved in his death. But when you showed me that photo of Jackie, I knew they were tangled up in something really bad. I guess they found me to be an issue. Otherwise, why would I be lying in this hospital bed."

"Did you talk with Jackie before you left for home the day you had your accident?" Trixie asked the question.

Stephanie's face showed concern as if she were thinking back to that day and found it difficult to remember just what happened. Her eyes squinted almost closing. "Yes, I spoke with Jackie. I told her you showed me her photo but I hadn't said anything about the plan she and Karen had hatched. I guess she didn't believe me. Was it Jackie who ran me down? I thought she was my friend." Trixie could feel the heartbreak in her words. Stephanie Sweet was a trusting soul. Too trusting it appeared.

"We don't know. We'll be asking that very question of Jackie soon. We don't know how she was involved. Maybe she wasn't," the detective tried to be gentle and assuring but Trixie knew he was certain of Jackie's guilt. They would soon find out the truth.

"You are now safe. We were concerned until now, but can be certain that you have nothing to fear," the detective patted her hand and rose to leave. As Trixie opened the door, she spotted Luke in the hallway holding a lovely bouquet of flowers. She smiled. Her stomach quaked with a sudden thought —

was Stephanie Sweet indeed innocent? As she met Luke's eyes, she certainly hoped Stephanie had been telling the truth. For his sake.

Walking back to the hotel to retrieve her few possessions from her room, she gazed at the lights flashing through the sky. Las Vegas was indeed exciting — maybe too exciting! She would have to check in on Tyra and Tino to see how they were faring after their performance. The detective walked along side Trixie and when they reached the entrance thanked her and nodded as he headed toward the security office. She knew without the plan to flush out the killer of Edward Garrett there would have been no evidence against Karen Danbury. Actually, other than the attempt on Tyra's life during the performance, Karen couldn't be linked to Edward's murder at all. Trixie frowned at the thought. Her phone buzzed in her jacket pocket.

"Oh, by the way." It was the detective. "Luz Maria identified Karen Danbury as the woman who took the meal cart from her in the hallway before Edward's murder. Just thought you might want to know that piece of information." She could almost see him shrugging on the other end of the phone.

"So I'm assuming you arranged for her green card," Trixie's voice trailed a bit with this statement.

He laughed. "Taken care of."

"Good. I feel much better," Trixie could see the image of the poor woman seated in her hotel room with her young daughter and felt relief.

"And we have a confession as well from Jackie Heidleman. She was the one who called in the meal order from Tyra's room. Karen slipped Tyra's key card from her bag when Tyra was shopping in Karen's booth the first day of the competition. Karen in turn gave Jackie the card to make the room service call. Then Jackie returned the card so Karen could slip the knife into Tyra's room after the murder. Jackie panicked when Stephanie told her about your visit with the photo of Jordan and followed Stephanie home. She couldn't risk Stephanie telling anyone about the connection between Jackie and Karen. That would raise a red flag. After she struck Stephanie, Jackie ran ditching the car along the way and hitchhiking to Jordan's apartment. Jordan didn't know about the plot to murder Edward and frame Tyra, but she will be charged with hiding a fugitive. She'll probably get off on that charge." Again Trixie could almost see the detective shrugging his shoulders on the other end of the phone. She smiled at the thought. He ended with, "I'll keep you informed as we investigate further."

"Thanks," Trixie mumbled and hung up the phone. In front of her checking out at the front desk were Tyra and Tino. Tyra was still in full make-up including her fluttering false eyelashes. The two of them were bantering back and forth arguing about charges to their rooms.

"What is this charge?" Tyra demanded pointing with a lengthy fingernail to an item on the list.

"A guy's got to eat!" Tino was screaming back as he dropped his black bag to the floor and crossed his arms.

"Meals were included in this competition package. Couldn't you just eat at the banquets and buffets provided? What do you have — a hollow leg? Where do you put all of this extra food? Ok. So who were you seeing? What young beauty were you trying to impress?" Tyra's voice became loud and agitated.

"Say what?" Tino put up his hands in defense but didn't sound that convincing. It almost sounded as if he were shocked he had gotten caught.

Trixie sighed. Hadn't this pair learned anything from this experience? Maybe Tyra was unaware of the reason her life had been in danger — the real reason Edward Garrett had lost his life. She, Trixie would have to have a nice little conversation with Tyra Fields when they returned to Minneapolis.

Trixie left the bantering pair and went to retrieve her bag running into Carl Friend at the elevator. He looked tired.

"Are you leaving?" he asked as she gave him a quick flutter of her fingers.

"I'm packing up right now. You?" She could see his bag in hand. He nodded. "Well, did the events of the competition release some old feelings or are they still there gnawing at your soul?"

Her question took Carl by surprise. For a moment he looked stunned and pondered his response. "I guess you're telling me to move on with my life and get over the past." He smiled slowly and stared back into her eyes.

"I would — if I were you. You've struggled too long with 'ago' and need to get to 'now'." She smiled back. "You have too much to give rather than to worry about what could have been."

"I've actually been a very fortunate man when I think about everything. I was given the opportunity to live in the world of dance, enjoy the world of dance, and share the world of dance with others. Maybe I should just look

201

forward rather than backward. Thank you for pointing it out to me. I know it is because you care — and I appreciate that." He smiled with a relief he hadn't shown the rest of the week and gave her a quick peck on the cheek. "See you later!"

Trixie knew she would indeed see him later. She watched him walk out of the hotel with a lightness to his step. Was that a whistle she heard? She couldn't tell over the continued argument between Tino and Tyra which was now drawing the attention of everyone in the lobby. Trixie quickly entered the elevator and enjoyed the silence. She was certain she would sleep all the way home. Back to Ashley Arthur in the morning! Who knows what adventure that would bring.

THE LAMBADA

The Lambada originates from Brazil so emulates various parts of several of the local Brazilian dances including the better known Samba. Popular in the 1980's, this dance is typically found in the night clubs with a smaller more intimate setting. Danced primarily in one spot, the Lambada moves from side to side with the legs bowed and the hips shaking. The partners typically dance close together with bent legs alternating — man's left leg, lady's right leg, man's right leg, and lady's left leg on the outside. The popular short skirts worn during that 1980's decade made the Lambada a very sensual dance — the forbidden dance as it was called.

www.ingramcontent.com/pod-product-compliance
Lightning Source LLC
Chambersburg PA
CBHW060736180626
46819CB00001B/44